JOSEPH ROY WRIGHT

SMALL TOWN HORRORS
THE NORTH WEST

Copyright Notice:

All the characters and events in this book are a work of fiction. Any Resemblances to real people, living or dead, or any events that may resemble any that have really happened are purely coincidental. First published and copyrighted by the author of this book Joseph Roy Wright in 2022. The author retains sole copyright to his or her contributions to this book.

Amazon's Kindle Direct Publishing service provided the layout design and graphic elements of this Self Published book. The author retains sole copyright to his or her contributions to this book.

Other Books
By Joseph Roy Wright

New Order of Alexnadria
Paranormal Homicide
The Town Named Bilmo
Realms of Solaride
Born Without Mothers

Table of Contents:

Introduction..5
Do not Enter..6
The Headless Horseman Of Halton Village...27
Horror Fair: The Stolen Children.........47
The North Witch.....................................60
Warrington Warriors.........................70
Frog Of Frodsham...........................78
Spike Island Spiders.......................94
Last Train Home...........................103
Demon Dogs Of Delamere....................116
Death On The Mersey.......................123
Afterword.................................143
Acknowledgements..........................145
Horror Book Previews......................146
Realms Of Solaride – Preview..............147
Paranormal Homicide – Preview.............154
The Town Named Bilmo – Preview............163

Introduction:

This is a series of short anthology horror stories by British author Joseph Roy Wright from Runcorn, Cheshire. He is a independent author who has written six self-published novels; *New Order Of Alexandria, Paranormal Homicide, The Town Named Bilmo, Realms Of Solaride, Born Without Mothers* and *Small Town Horrors*. This new book series will explore fictional horror stories based off real places and urban legends that exist around the UK. This first Volume; *Small Town Horrors: The North West* will take inspiration from haunted locations, abandoned places and local myths from places around the north west of England, where the author is from. All of the stories presented here are fictional. Nothing here is meant to be taken too seriously. So enjoy this collection of horror stories! From the supernatural to murder mysteries, *Small Town Horrors* is full of genuine terror that will keep you up for many years to come.

Do not enter

Some years ago two teenagers went urban exploring inside the abandoned apartments besides Runcorn's shopping centre. These buildings have stood untouched for almost 10 years and plans to refurbish them have come and gone like tears in the rain. The site is unsafe and there are many signs all over the place that state:

"DO NOT ENTER"

Yet, these two teens decided to go against the rules anyway and what they found inside would haunt them for life! They were somewhat wise, as they only dared venture inside at the dead of night, when the shopping centre had shut and nobody was around.
'This is perfect...' Danny snickered as he and his friend Sam, climbed up the steel, red painted staircase that was a mess with graffiti. Sam was filming the whole thing on his mobile phone, they planned on uploading the video online afterwards. Even with the old street lights everywhere, their surroundings

were dark and a cool, damp mist surrounded them, as it had been raining a few minutes ago.

'I don't think this is a good idea, Dan...' Sam gulped as he stared at the barb wire that Danny was snipping away at, with his mother's kitchen knife from home. These two were way over their heads thinking that this was a good idea, Danny saw some viral videos online about abandoned places and haunted buildings with millions of views, he wanted in on that publicity. Not for money, but just for fame, Danny wanted to go viral because it was trendy. He thought the other kids in school would think he was awesome! They did this on a Saturday night when it was somewhat normal for teens their age to be out and about late. That way, their parents would be none the wiser. Sam didn't want to do any of this! It was Danny's idea and he was just being roped along into it. Sam wouldn't have dared do this if it wasn't for his hyper active friend, who always got him into trouble with stupid pranks. Deep down inside, Sam envied his friend Danny, as he was the cool kid in school. He was dating Amy, the "Dream Girl" everyone called her and Sam just wanted to be a part of the cool club. Despite Danny's popularity, nobody was dumb enough to follow him into the abandoned apartments, apart from Sam of course. You see, Sam was a little on the chubby side and he was shorter too, a year younger than Danny, he only just squeezed into the same class as him by a mere 3 months. Most of the kids were 15, while he was still 14. Danny may have only been a few months older than Sam, but he was always reminded how "he was only 14" and he struggled to relate with his classmates too. Sam was very desperate to fit in, which is why he went along with Danny's stupid "adventure" as he would call it. 'Don't be such a pussy, Sam...' Danny mocked, while cutting the barb wire. 'Think about all the views we'd be getting! We'll be famous, lad. Coolest kids around!' He laughed. Danny was quite naive, so used to getting his way all the time, he honestly thought this video would make him a super star! Sam felt like this was dumb, but Danny was almost a bully more than a friend to Sam, he was just manipulating him with

promises of being popular.
'We're gonna make it bi- Oh shit!' Danny
cried in pain.
'What's the matter?!' Sam gasped. Danny
held up his bare hand, there was an ugly
flesh wound across his palm and blood
leaked out, relentlessly.
'Cut my fucking hand, that's what!'
Danny yelled, fiercely.
'Well, maybe we better forget about this
then, eh?' Sam sighed with relief as he
turned the camera off his phone and put
it away.
'Keep rolling!' Danny roared.
'Oh, all right!' Sam yelped and began
recording again.
'I'll just wrap my sock around it... for
now.' Danny sighed, before placing his
knife down and sitting on the rain
soaked floor. He removed his white
trainer, pulled his sock off his foot
and painfully wrapped it round his
bleeding hand. 'See...' Danny smiled,
holding up his sock wrapped hand.
'...good as new!' He winked. 'Now, let's
go into the ABANDONED APARTMENTS!' He
laughed into the camera, making a creepy
voice (this was "entertainment" for the
online video). Even Sam chuckled and

after a few minutes, Danny began re-cutting the barb wire again. They made enough room to get through and entered the dark, abandoned apartments.

They crept in through a tiny entrance, that was blocked off mostly with wooden boards that were intended to keep people out, not in! Of course, Sam got stuck on the way inside, half his body wouldn't budge passed the splintered wood that was digging, sharply into his tender flesh, cutting apart his expensive t-shirt and track suit. He groaned in pain, while Danny laughed.
'Come on, lad!' He mocked.
'I can't... get through!' Sam cried. Before he could react, Danny began stabbing the wooden boards in front of him, violently. Sam screamed in terror, while Danny laughed like a maniac, breaking apart the wood like it was made of glass! Sam eventually broke free, fell on his hands and dropped the phone. Danny actually showed some rare kindness and offered to lift Sam up by his hand. Sam forced a smile and grabbed his friend's hand, Danny lifted him up, before brushing off the wooden splinters

off Sam's front. His shirt, tracksuit jacket and bottoms now had small holes all over them and there were cuts of blood all over Sam's body. However, they weren't deep, so they didn't sting too badly either. Danny picked up the phone and handed it back to Sam, he rolled his eyes as if to say; "Really? After all that!" Danny chuckled and patted Sam on the back.

'The worst is over now lad, let's just do a quick video and then we can leave, eh?' Danny suggested.

'All right mate, let's have a look around...' Sam reluctantly agreed.

'Boss lad!' Danny winked, 'bit too dark in here, ain't it? Luckily, I got a torch on me. Put on the torch app on your phone too, Sam...' Danny ordered and Sam obliged. Now they had two sources of light, but even still, it was almost impossible to see ten foot in front of them. The inside of this place was creepy and ghostly. An ice cold air breezed through the empty hallways and the walls were a ruin with mould, decay and flaked paint. Both friends found this place to be really cool, "Just like a found footage movie!" They both remarked. Sam filmed the area with wonder, aiming the camera at the blackened ceiling, the dismantled furniture and the rats and birds that fled away from them. Insects squirmed under fallen chairs, shelves and tables. There was a small hint of asbestos that hung in the air, which would've made any sensible adult know that this place was toxic. Unfortunately, the stupid teens didn't know any better! Foolishly, they entered further into this darkness. The floors, doors and even walls creaked as they ventured through the claustrophobic corridors. They ventured through each room and found graffiti everywhere, which obviously implied that they weren't the only ones to enter. Danny was still smug however, feeling as though nobody dared film inside this place before.

'Man... this video is going to be fire!' Danny cheered and the sound sent birds and maybe even bats flying from the roof, the sudden motion of several animals caused the ceiling to shake.

'Oh shit!' Sam screamed, as the debris began to crumble above them, they both stood back quickly and watched as the

roof caved in and crashed before them.
They were lucky to escape the fall, and
watched in horror and amazement.
'Please tell me, you got that on
camera!' Danny laughed in shock.
'Yeah...' Sam held up his phone '...just
about!' Their way forward was blocked
and after that near death experience
(and awesome video footage for Danny),
they were both satisfied to leave. There
was no way they could climb upwards and
onto the roof, so they turned back to go
out the way they came and Sam was still
rolling. They walked slowly back to the
doorway, being careful not to cause any
more disruptions.
'Oh my god!' Danny gasped and pointed,
Sam turned the camera and saw the blur
of a man, or something else run passed
the doorway, slamming the door in front
of them, trapping them in the tight
corridor. They could hear the mysterious
stranger's footsteps fade away behind
the walls around them, followed by a
sinister snicker. Both lads stood
silently, pissing themselves in fear.
They didn't say a word and just froze.
Eventually Sam breathed.
'We've got to get out of here...' Danny

whispered.

'Ye-yeah...' Sam agreed. After waiting a few minutes, they eventually gathered the courage to sneak into the only nearby room (or at least what remained of one anyway) to the left of them. At this point, Sam had completely forgotten about recording the video and Danny no longer cared either. However, the phone was safely hidden in Sam's pocket and the footage they had collected was still saved on the device, not that they cared any more anyway. The inside of this room was hideous, there was an old sofa with rats on top of it, they scattered upon the boy's entry. An old CRT television lay on it's side, busted by either the stranger, rats or somebody else. One thing was for sure; they weren't the first to enter this abandoned place. They didn't dare sit down on that brown smeared sofa, so they just stood around hopelessly, feeling trapped with no place safe to go!

'We'll just have to wait this out...' Danny suggested with a worried sigh.

'Yeah, hopefully that stranger fucks off!' Sam snapped, loudly.

'Calm down, you tit!' Danny panicked.

'You want him to hear us?' he asked, rhetorically. Sam sighed heavily and leant against a wall. He brought out his phone and used the torch app to see more clearly.

'Stop that!' Danny snapped. Sam sighed again and turned the app off. They stood in that silent living room for a while. Eventually, Sam announced he was going to use the ensuite toilet. Danny shrugged as he was far too focused on thinking about an escape route. Sam stepped lightly through the living room, looking for the ensuite, being careful not to alert the mysterious stranger again. A foul odour came from the door he presumed led to the toilet, he gulped and took a deep breath before foolishly forcing himself to enter. The door was heavy, so he gave it a hard push and a fresh body crashed onto the ground in front of him, making a soft but loud thud. Sam screamed, Danny flew into the ensuite and revolted in horror. Somebody had been murdered! It was a girl, young and small, not much older than they were. The boys cried quietly, trying to remain hidden, but it was no use. However the killer only snickered, barely audible behind the walls, but evidently there like some phantom ghost, the monster lingered.

'What are we going to do?!' Danny whined.

'You and your stupid pranks!' Sam roared, 'look what you've got us into!' he pointed at the dead body, who's eyes moved.

'Help...' the dead girl whimpered.

'You're alive?!' Danny gasped.

'Only barely...' Sam breathed, 'look how beaten and scarred she is, she's only just hanging on!'

'Oh my god...' Danny cried. This girl was severely beaten, bloodied and covered in wounds. She smelt like death, she looked like it too, but she still lingered on. The attack was recent, but there was no saving her, as she bled like a tap. Soon she closed her eyes for good and truly slept forever, while the boys just stared, powerless and clueless to stop her demise.

They returned to the living room. 'Whatever will we d-' Sam stopped. He stared in disbelief, for a tall man, built like a brick wall and covered in blood, stood in the living room. His body language suggested that he was happy, but you couldn't truly tell, for he wore a black, old gas mask and a thick jacket made of brown leather. The stranger leered his head from one side to the other, before brandishing a long, sharp knife from behind his back. He danced from side to side, chuckling as he juggled the large knife from one hand to the other, like a circus clown; he put on a horrifying show that left the boys breathless. Danny grabbed Sam's hand and snatched him away towards the door, exiting the room and onto the corridor, foot steps from the masked lunatic followed behind and more birds or bats flew from the ceiling above them, causing more debris to fall.

'Run little boys, but there is no escape, for you too are already dead!' The stranger laughed, gleefully. They could hear him dancing behind them as the foot steps got louder. Sam barged for the door, but it wouldn't fall down, so he fiddled with the door knob, but it wouldn't budge!

'Come on Sam, hurry up!' Danny pleaded. A squelch and a thud hit Sam's ears, followed by a horrified scream. The stranger's knife was now pinned through Danny's hand and into the door. Danny cried, trying to free the knife, he kept screaming with every touch and with every jolt to get his hand free. His now red face, a mess with tears!

'We're not going to make it, we're not going to make it, we're not going to make it!' Danny wailed in pain, sorrow and terror!

'Shut up, shut up!' Sam screamed, hurting his throat. His vision was blurred with tears and the dark didn't help either, he could barely see a thing, just noises and colours of pure fear and turmoil. He blinked several times, clearing away his tears, his vision returned just before the knife was yanked back out and sliced into Danny's throat. A splash of blood hit Sam's face, he blinked again and again until he saw Danny choking, then the knife pierced through his friend's skull. Danny's face and body dropped dead in front of him. When Danny fell, his body was pushed to one side, in his wake stood the gas masked man, covered in blood, 'You're next!'

Sam awoke! Was it all a dream? He wasn't truly sure, for his body was in pain, but it had been for a long time, 5 years in fact. The facts were coming back together, he was still lost within that night terror, slowly waking up to his true hell. He remembered now, and suddenly the nightmare seemed like a dream compared to his reality. For you see, Danny and Sam really did go into those abandoned apartments, only there was no killer, well not a human one anyway. Nor was it any animal, but a threat non the less real, only it was invisible and far more insidious. No, not a ghost or even a spirit, but a toxin that hung in the air. It was the asbestos that killed Danny, only last year. They had been suffering from it for years after that foolish night in Runcorn. None of them knew the dangers of the toxic gas until it was too late! Of all the things they teach in school, avoiding asbestos was not one of them (maybe it was in some science class, but they never cared to remember). Sam didn't want to believe it! So, he tried to stand, but only puked blood and struggled to breathe. He shook around the hospital bed like a fish out of water, quickly dying as he could no longer breathe. A nurse overheard, she casually walked in only to jump into a panic and grab the breathing mask from the side of his bed, placing it tightly around Sam's mouth. He fell asleep again shortly, but he didn't dream this time.

He awoke a few hours later and the same nurse removed his mask.
'Feel any better?' She asked.
'Ye- yes...' Sam breathed heavily, struggling to speak. It was like his air ways were blocked with tar. The invisible killer still strangling him to this day, the knife cutting away at his throat, until he too was dead, just like Danny. Sam had no idea how long he had left, yet he lingered on, hoping for a cure.
'Doctor Smith is still looking over the analysis from yesterday, he'll let you know soon enough how well you are doing. Just take it easy, Sam.'
'It- it's no... use...' Sam cried painfully.
'Now don't say that!' The nurse smiled,

her pretty face was a treat. 'This is curable and there is treatment. You've lasted this long Sammy, so don't give up.'

'I... won't.' He forced a smile, but he knew deep down that this wasn't going to end well.

Many hours passed and all Sam could do was think about what happened all those years ago. Just like in the dream, the debris really fell, trapping them inside. There was no dead girl in the ensuite and no gas mask killer either. However the asbestos lingered around all three of them, yes there was another; Amy. The "Dream Girl" was with them and she already had asthma before entering. They couldn't get through the door exiting the premises either, as it had broken upon their arrival. So they waited inside all night and morning, banging on the windows that wouldn't smash open as wooden boards blocked their exit. Amy was dying quickly with a panic attack too, she couldn't breathe at all, Sam and Danny didn't know what to do, so she died in front of them. Danny cried and they moved the body into

the ensuite once she began to stink. In the late morning, they heard a passer-by walking, so Danny and Sam screamed for help and the rescuer soon came to their aid, risking but saving his and their lives in the process. However, Amy's death still haunted them for years and the asbestos in their lungs was here to stay. They were both hospitalised after a year and hated each other for a while, but at least they weren't to die alone. Until Danny passed away, of course.
'There you are!' Doctor Smith walked into the hospital room, smiling.
'Not like... I-I'm go-going any... where.' Sam replied.
'No, of course not...' Doctor Smith paused, unsure of himself. Sam was beyond annoyed with this man's clumsiness and snapped his fingers to get him to read the analysis. Doctor Smith's smile suddenly turned into a frown. He took a deep breath and almost teared up before composing himself. Sam cried before Doctor Smith had time to speak. He knew it was over.

That night, just before Sam was about to sleep, the hospital room's door creaked open. He opened his eyes wide and looked. A bloodied hand crept around the door frame and a gas mask peered in from within the darkness, followed by that sinister chuckle. Sam froze, but he couldn't move much anyway, as the gas mask killer crept closer, he began to wheeze in panicked breaths. The murderer danced eloquently across the hospital room and reached out with both hands to grasp Sam's neck. Sam could see the killer's eyes light up beneath that mask of horror, as his muffled laughter became more apparent. There was nothing Sam could do, not even scream, for his lungs were tightening as the gas mask killer squeezed his hands around Sam's neck. He kicked and threw his body around to escape, but the murderer was overwhelming and too strong for Sam to handle. He leant into Sam's body, pressing his hands down harder, meaner and tighter around the 19 year old's jugular. His eyes locked with the killer, a look of pure terror on Sam's face as it turned red, then purple before finally sleeping forever. The gas mask killer stood up and cheerfully bowed over Sam's body. As the beeping from the life support machine dinged rapidly, the lights snapped on and several Doctors and Nurses raced into the room to try and save poor Sam's life. The invisible killer stood in the corner watching, the hospital staff couldn't do a thing, no matter how much CPR they did, no matter how many Doctors and Nurses screamed and stuck tubes and other medical equipment down Sam's throat there really was no saving him. The ghost laughed loudly and nobody heard a thing, for Sam's brain was still barely active and only he could hear this menace snicker in delight. Eventually the sounds faded and there was nothing left of Sam, but a motionless body that died.

'The illness unfortunately...' Doctor Smith sighed, trying to be formal, but even he teared when he saw Sam's mother's face.
'...passed away!' She cried into her hands. He stood still for a moment, allowing her to grieve. 'Wha- what happened?' She asked. Doctor Smith hesitated.
'Are you sure you want to know?'

'Yes!' She snapped, 'Just tell me...'
'Ok...' he sighed, 'Your son had been having several night terrors over the last weeks. Sam would awake in a panic, choking and wheezing for air and we would have to aid him back to health. He told us of a gas masked man, hunting him down and his friend Danny, inside the abandoned apartments near Runcorn's shopping centre.'
'He was still having that same nightmare?' Sam's mother cried.
'I'm afraid so...' Doctor Smith sighed deeply, 'for the past months now, the night terrors were coming and going, but they came back strong and unfortunately as these series of fits escalated, his health deteriorated. I am sorry Danielle Connor, we tried everything to save him...'
'You could've done better!' She snapped, 'Couldn't you have done something to ease his pain, stop these nightmares?'
'I'm afraid not, we're deeply sorry, but there was no way of stopping this. Drugs, sedatives or pain killers could dull Sam's pain during the day, but there was nothing we could've done while he was sleeping.' The Doctor explained.

Danielle stared in silence, crying quietly. At least Sam's nightmares were finally over.

The Headless Horseman of Halton Village

Monday – 9/5/22:

Throughout the years, many have speculated the existence of ghosts and spirits. Is there an afterlife? Is death really the end, or do we still linger on as lost spirits. These questions can never truly be answered. You either believe in the occult, find it nonsensical or you are somewhere in-between, entirely unsure whether or not the supernatural exists. Well, an old friend of mine, Andrew Bates, would tell you it's all real! He first encountered his greetings with the undead, all the way back in 2001, a good 21 years ago when he was just a young boy in school. This was during that infamous murder case known as: *The Skinner's Incident*, where a killer was going around town, skinning people alive! It was sick, but many (including Andrew) dared say that the killer had a paranormal origin. He even wrote a independent novel based off the events titled *Paranormal Homicide: The Skinner's Incident*, which was quickly pulled off shelves in 2019 as it was seen as insensitive and offensive to those who were truly involved. However whenever I mention this to him, he proclaims that; "This was all real and that the demon tormented him first, appearing as a black skeletal creature, with multiple wings and limbs like a Spider-Bat!". It all sounded so ridiculous, even I doubted his sanity. There is one case however that is still fresh on all of our minds. The case which involved several mysterious be-headings near the areas of Halton Castle. This first began in 2011 a good 10 years after the bizarre murders in Runcorn and again; police were completely dumbfounded by the series of killings. No evidence to point fingers, they seemed to happen at random and I even met a woman who said she saw her boyfriend's head tear off by itself and fall to the ground in front of her, like some phantom ghost had chopped the man's head off with an invisible sword. Many who dared walk by the castle around 1-3am would sometimes be found beheaded and others have claimed to see a skeletal horse and headless knight in black, chase them around the castle grounds. These killings stopped by 2012 and nobody has mentioned the headless horseman since. Yet I've often heard echoes of a horse clattering across the castle grounds at night and some have even heard a man speak in old English screaming things like; "I strike thee!", "Ye all dead!" and "Have at it, fools!". Many find these bizarre occurrences to be humorous, but there is certainly a dark undertone to all of this. On some quiet mornings when nobody is around, I've heard many say that you can almost hear the faint war cries of ancient warriors battling over the castle and many say this ends with a horrifying scream that only lasts ten seconds, the same time a headless man is still conscious, before dying. Very creepy stuff, but it's hard to say if it's all just our imaginations playing tricks on us, being fully aware of the horrifying myth that surrounds the place. I'm fairly new to this town, only moving here in 2020 after the pandemic, I had to move somewhere cheap and settled into the Runcorn old town. I'll have to ask Andrew more about this when I next see him, for he's lived here all his life and he claims to be a psychic. As you probably guessed.

Sunday - 15/5/22:

So I spoke to Andrew. I think he may be nuts! He said; "I helped hide the headless horseman away from harming anyone again". He was drinking with me in the Kings Bar of Runcorn old town and at first he was vague about the whole mystery.

"Yes, the headless horseman exists, and he still haunts Halton Castle and sometimes it's surrounding areas..." He began.

"Really, the legends ring true?"

"Uh huh..." He sighed and sat in silence, drinking his pint. Listening to the music. I needed to buy him a few drinks to loosen his tongue. He knew what I was doing, but welcomed the free shots and drinks regardless. He lay back in his booth, sighing with relief, he was happily drunk and looked at me with a slight smile.

"11 years ago; the ghost manifested. For whatever reason, the monster could do harm. Reach people, grab them, hurt them, he killed some! Much like the demon from 2001, we had another supernatural killer on our hands. How do I know all this? I'm a psychic, you see?" Andrew winked, tapping his forehead.

"I know. You told me that already, Andrew."

"I did?" He chuckled, "I tell everyone. Some think I'm a creep, but whatever... I'm an unsung hero, Jessica. Nobody knows it, but I've saved a lot of lives from these undead scum!" He groaned, going off topic. I felt sorry for this bloke, in his early thirties and a bit of a loner, luckily I found the rumours surrounding Runcorn's hauntings to be intriguing and not disturbing. So I pressed him further and he gathered his thoughts. "You want to know how we stopped him, huh?" He cut straight to the point.

"Yes!" I smiled, finally relieved to get some answers.

"I've met a lot of other psychics too, you see? There are more of us than just me, in this town alone. There are also some, much like yourself, who may not have connections to the underworld, but believe in it all none the less. The

connections linked, the multiple paranormal homicides were all related, invisible be-headings around the same parts of Halton Village, spreading further and further away from the castle. The ghost was growing in strength, slowly becoming an unstoppable serial killer of occult origin. We tracked him down to his death place, inside the castle. We summoned him with a biblical ritual and all of us fought with weapons and fists to stop the headless knight and his skeletal horse! A few of us died..." Andrew cried. I sat in silence and in awe, even some of the other bar guests moved seats or stared in disgust at us both for his bizarre tales. "Nobody believes me." He said, his face still full of tears. "Do you?"
"I don't know..." I was honest. He chuckled, sarcastically.
"I can show you..." He grinned creepily.
"...H-how?" I dared ask.
"Show you a vision." He said, "Prove it to you. That what I say is true. I warn you though, Jessica... what you will see, you can't un-see! The horrors I see on a daily basis would drive you mad. To me, it's normal now to see the undead

walk among us, like lost zombies. However you may be traumatised by the horrors of the second sight..." He spoke much quieter now, that of a whisper. I listened intently. "Are you busy tomorrow?" He asked me.

"No... I'm free." I hesitated. My curiosity was getting the better of me, but I was far too invested now to walk away. Deep down, I felt like Andrew was really a good guy, just deeply misunderstood. Maybe I was wrong, thoughts of him being the true serial killer crept into my mind. Was it him that "beheaded" all those people?! I wanted to doubt it, so I bit the bullet. "At 11:30pm tomorrow, we must meet at Halton Castle. For this vision to work, it must be midnight!"

"Why midnight?" I asked.

"Because... nobody is around." He chuckled, "Well, truth is, these things always work better before dawn on a silent night like Sunday..."

"But why?"

"Who am I, god?!" Andrew laughed sharply, "I don't why, it just is... So, Jessica, are you in?"

"I'm in!" With that, our conversation

ended. We went our separate ways. Now I'm home alone, writing this blog about my investigation into the mystery of the headless horseman. Andrew is my final lead, digging deeper into this rabbit hole of death and horror. I only hope I'm right about Andrew and that he's not some psycho. Wish me look I guess. It's almost midnight!

Monday - 16/5/22:

I'm lucky to be alive. Seriously. Not that I had a near death experience, but I've seen the other side and it's not pretty! I met Andrew last night outside Halton castle, he had a black leather bound book with him and a rather large salt shaker, I was as much amused as I was terrified. Why did he have such strange items with him? I approached him with caution, those serial killer vibes becoming more and more alarming. Andrew smiled and beckoned me to come over, his friendly persona over powered me and I immediately felt at ease. He laughed when I got near.
"It's not me, that you should be afraid of..." he whispered under his breath, which instantly unsettled me again,

before he led me up the creepy castle's staircase, into the yard, where nobody was around, but me, him and the unholy ghost! I remember trembling with sweat, as the rumours and myths began to ring true. I could subtly hear ancient warriors scream and fight around me, it was hard to listen under the wind of rustled trees and grass, but evidently there, like the legends had said. It ended with a scream that echoed across half of Runcorn, for only 10 seconds before an abrupt stop. Silence. Andrew grinned, looking me in the eyes. "Now do you believe me?" He asked. I did. "I can show you more..." Andrew continued, holding open his hand. I bit my lip, stared at him, contemplating whether or not this was a good idea. Again, I jumped down the rabbit hole, falling deeper into an abyss, my world grew dark around me!

I was blinded by the bright red sky. My eyes readjusted with the environment and it seemed like I was in a different realm. I charged for a warrior, while riding my trusty steed! The Safrons were invading Castle Riverfall, and it was up to me, and a band of knights to protect our home!

"I strike thee!" I roared at the warrior, destroying our barricade, piercing him with my lance, straight through the chest! Blood shot out everywhere!

"Ye all dead!" Another Safron warrior screamed, hatchet in hand, charging for me!

"Have at it, fools!" I mocked and readied myself for another assault, but the hatchet warrior whacked my horse, she yelped in terror and threw me off her back. I rolled to a halt, the strong beast of a man, ran to my side and before I could equip my sword, he slashed for my neck. I felt the tenants in my jugular snap, crack and tear apart before I screamed in complete agony, my head spinning in the air, my motionless body beheaded in front me! I rolled to a stop, this time without my body. A trail of blood and gore lay across the battle ground, where I had been beheaded.

"What the fuck!" I screamed, waking up from that nightmare!
"Quite the thrill, huh?!" Andrew

laughed, tensed and shaken, just like me.

"Wha-what was that?!" I stuttered, waking up from that night terror, of be-headings, battles and blades slicing away at tender flesh, feeling the agony of my neck stripping away from it's body!

"That's how the headless horseman of Halton village died..." Andrew winked. I snatched away my hand from his. "I told you things would never be the same." He said.

"Don-don't you touch me!" I cried, backing away from him frantically, stumbling over my feet, crashing onto the once blood soiled ground.

"Ah shit!" Andrew trembled. "Shit, shit, shit!" He screamed and I ran. Then I hit invisible metal, head first into nothing, but a pain I still remember bounced back into my mind and I almost fell down, but Andrew caught me, saving my fall.

"Wha-What happened?" I asked, dazed and confused.

"He's back!" Andrew gasped, pointing ahead of me.

"What, where, who... Oh my god!" I

couldn't believe it, Headless Horseman was appearing before us. I was soon to learn why Andrew brought his book and salt shaker.

"Stand back!" He ordered, pulling me up to his side, before pushing himself in front to protect me. The headless horseman approached, slowly but with menace!

"You awake me, now fear my might!" A rotten head screamed at me, I spun, crying in fear! It smiled, worms coming out of the mouth. Andrew kicked it away like a football, hitting the armoured monster. I heard another laugh, but it wasn't the headless horseman, it was his skeletal horse, marching towards us from seemingly nowhere. Mist stalked in around us, trapping us in-between these two beasts. Two mortals; a man and a woman, versus two monsters from beyond the grave.

"This can't be real, this is just a dream, a nightmare!" I laughed hysterically, losing my mind.

"This isn't a dream, Jessica, this is really happening!" Andrew roared, holding me back, stopping me from escaping. I tried to fight him, but

looking back on it; he was only trying to protect me. "I'm not your enemy, Jessica. They are!" He pointed at the monsters. I held my chest and breathed heavily, in a fit of panic. Andrew picked up his salt shaker, that was laying beside his feet. He drew a salt circle around us, which only made me feel even more trapped, but I had to trust him, I had no choice. The fiery eyed skeleton horse charged for us, then reared away from the salt that burned it's skull into dark ash. It kicked and screamed madly, as it's body turned to ember, burning away in a horrifying blaze of green and blue fire, leaving behind a trail of black ash that was once a horrifying demon. Now only the headless knight stood, inches away from us, never daring to enter our circle of safety. Andrew took the book from his pocket and ruthlessly flipped through the pages, looking for the right passage.
"Not again, thou shalt not defile me, Andrew Bates of Runcorn!" The screaming head boomeranged back, zooming through the air towards us! Headless Horseman cried as his head burned into a ball of

fire, entering our circle, knocking me to the ground and out of the barrier. The burning head now lay face to face with mine.

"You're fucked!" It laughed hysterically, as it's already rotten flesh boiled away until it was nothing but a blackened skull that turned to ash. I looked up for help, but the headless knight slammed his sword down, aiming for my neck!

"Jessica!" Andrew cried, pulling me back into the circle, mere seconds before I too was beheaded.

"I've got the passage!" He cheered, before reciting it: "With the power of God and the holy ghost, lords give me strength against this foul demon!" With this, the knight retorted, pacing around the circle with desperation, trying to scare us out.

"No use, fool!" A surrounding voice echoed, it was as if the mist itself was alive and barking at us.

"Back to hell, you unholy fiend, the power of Christ compels you!" Andrew roared, confidently.

"Fuck you, you're both little cunts! A place in hell awaits thee!" The mist

laughed, fearfully as the ground began to shake. We struggled to stay inside the circle! The headless knight hit the ground with his sword, trying to dig under the salt and be-head us!
"Christ give me strength, send this foul beast back!" Andrew groaned, not even looking in the book, I was sure he was making that bit up out of desperation and frustration. Obviously it didn't work, as the mist's laughter became deafening, closing in around us, until our vision was unclear, only the shadows and silhouette of the headless knight remained, his sword stabbing through the white blanket of mist every now and again. Black clouds appeared within this mist, taking on the shapes of contorted faces, all moaning out in agony.
"More lost souls for my collection! You mortal bastards shall soon suffer eternal torment. Sucking cocks in hell!" Mist roared again, as the knight's sword dashed in and out of the circle, always close enough to hit us.
"The power of Christ compels you!" Andrew stood fiercely, raging against the dark. "Go back to where you once came! I take this holy stance, the

powers of God, Christ and the holy ghost compels you!" He roared loudly, deafening even me. The mist began to clear and the headless knight was thrown back by an invisible rugby tackle, but the ghost still lingered no matter how much he screamed, chanted and raged! Soon the knight and mist crowded in on us again, as Andrew grew tired losing this fight. He looked at me, trying to figure out what was wrong.
"You're scared!" He roared, angrily.
"I ca-can't hel-help it!" I stuttered in fear, crying my eyes out.
"That's what's keeping him here! You mustn't fear the reaper!"
"I'm afraid he'll kill us, lock us in hell, forever in torment!" I screamed hysterically and the sword dashed back into the circle again as our vision became nothing but white smoke.
"It's fear that's keeping him here, stand with me!" He ordered, holding out his hand, which was warm to the touch. I held on and his strength launched through me, warming my heart and filling me with courage! I stood with him and faced the demon, with this, the mist feared away, but the headless knight

still stood.
"Chant with me, Jessica. It's the only way we can both defeat this evil!" Andrew smiled, looking into my eyes, before pointing me towards the book. We sung together, a choir of victory, diminishing the mist before the knight was sent running. He ran away, fearfully, vanishing into nothingness. The headless horseman was defeated.

Sunday - 22/5/22:

It has been a whole week since we sent the headless horseman back to hell. I didn't want to know Andrew at all after that night, but there were too many questions left unanswered, so I got back in touch. We met again last night in the Kings Bar. Andrew wasn't drunk this time, our friendship and trust had gone far passed drunken confessions. We met in the day when it was quiet, so there weren't too many drunks or idiots around to over hear.
"You want to know where the headless horseman came from?" He asked me, sitting back, comfortably into his cushioned seat.
"What was with the red sky during his

battle with the Safrons?" I asked and Andrew paused, taking a long, deep gulp of his pint of lager.

"We don't believe the headless horseman was from our realm."

"Who is we and what realm?" I asked.

"That's just the question, isn't it?" He chuckled, "A place where the sky bleeds red and knights become demons upon death. It certainly isn't from our earthling history... and we are an underground club of psychics and paranormal investigators. I told you that bit already, how it was us that originally sent him back. I didn't think he'd return so easily last week, I am sorry for that, Jess..." He apologised and I nodded, accepting his apology.

"So you have no idea where that place was?"

"We've got ideas. Some of us think it was hell, because of the red sky, but I think that's too obvious and I doubt hell has the freedom to fight for your kingdom. Others believe it's a supernatural realm named Solaride or a glimpse into the underworld, where the spirits of the undead roam free. Perhaps it was actually Runcorn, only hundreds of centuries ago in a time so far back we don't even know. I mean, seriously, all we know about the past is from history books, old buildings and artefacts. Nobody today is alive to say for certain whether or not everything we see, hear or know about our past is for certain. Maybe the sky was once a permanent red in the early 1000s, it may sound ridiculous, but nobody is around to say any different. I believe maybe these myths and legends of orcs and goblins, ghosts and spirits, giants and dragons actually stem from fact. However in this day and age, to believe in such madness would be seen as lunacy. I don't know what it is with our modern age, but these supernatural occurrences have become less common. Yet we do hear odd little tales here or there of hauntings and ghost sightings, I believe these paranormal events are echoes from the past, when monsters did roam the land. Perhaps one day, hell will rise once again and monsters will roam the lands." Andrew finished with a snicker. "... Or maybe I am just crazy..." he sighed. "I don't think you're crazy, Andrew..." I smiled, holding his hand. He looked

into my eyes, before reaching for his
pint and taking another gulp.
"I'm glad you don't think I'm crazy,
Jessica." He smiled back and snuggled in
closer to me, I held him, lovingly. The
people of Runcorn can say he's nuts all
they want, but he sure did make a
believer out of me.

Horror Fair: The Stolen Children

I was just 14 years old when I was abducted by the evil pirate ring master, Jipido, before he transformed me into the "Ancient Fortune Teller!" of Pirate Cove's travelling circus & funfair. I still remember when it happened, in every vivid, painful and humiliating detail.

It happened on a Friday night of 1913, it was summer and I was enjoying the Pirate Cove funfair with my father and older brother. This was in Widnes, but they were a travelling circus around Halton entertaining and, sadly, stealing children, turning them into circus freaks! I wouldn't have laughed at the freak show if I knew they were all once innocent kids. I ventured behind stage when the show had finished, my foolish childish curiosity getting the better of me. I slithered through the red curtains behind stage when everyone was gone, only to shortly be confronted with the evil ring master himself, Jipido. "Ahoy, what are yee doing back here!" He chuckled. I was immediately startled, but charmed by the performer's character. I giggled. "Argh! Why yee laughing, lass?" The eye patched pirate asked, shaking his hook in the air. He had the whole get up, a long grey beard, a pirate's hat and brown coat, with stockings tucked into his black leather boots.

"You're a funny character, that's all!" I grinned in excitement. Jipido snarled.

"Tis not a character, young lassie... I am a real pirate!" He grunted, but I still thought he was joking. "Here..." He removed his hook from his left forearm, "...let me show yer..." A purple snake without a face squirmed out of his hook, followed by three other smaller tentacles. Before I could scream, the pirate's alien limbs wrapped themselves around my head, neck and mouth. I screamed internally, I thought this was a nightmare, but it wasn't. "Now... What will I do tee yee?" Jipido said thoughtfully, removing his eye-patch to reveal a bright gold eye of hypnotism. I was immediately drawn into this eye of fire and cruelty, powerless to stop myself from mindlessly gazing into this golden abyss. He still held his tentacles around my upper body, but I was far too entranced to continue struggling. "I knows a terrific position for yee!" Jipido snickered, "We don't have many a fortune tellers around Pirate Cove, yee see? So, how's about this then: I make yer ancient and have ya telling folks their futures, you'd love that wouldn't yee?" He asked me, rhetorically.

"Yes. I'd love that." I replied blankly, but it was not what I wanted to say! In my mind, I screamed, cried and begged for escape. However the power this pirate had over me was overwhelming, I was soon to learn that this was no ordinary hypnotism. Those normally hypnotised must at least be open to the suggestion, yet with Jipido's supernatural talents, it didn't matter how much I denied or feared this concept. It was more like he took control of my sub conscious, depriving me of main thought.

"Hooray me hearty! young lass, I make ye an old witch!" He cheered before tightening his purple snakes tighter around my whole body, yet I just lay down limp, unable to wake. I could feel my skin shrink old and weathered, my bones grew, then thinned down to a frail crisp, making me short again. My eye sight faded into a clouded blur, my body ached like after a heavy workout and my heart tightened, making me feel sick and weak. You will never know the terrifying agony that went through my mind, as he forever morphed me into this grotesque image. After this was done, he loosened his tentacles' grasp around my body and released me, I was free, but not from his power. I struggled to stand, waking up from the hypnotism. It felt like a bad dream, or nightmare. So I first awoke relieved, thinking I would be back in bed, almost forgetting what had just happened. However my vision wouldn't unclear, but I could still see well enough to know that Jipido was still standing there, grinning at me. "N-no..." I croaked, not recognising my own voice, for it had deteriorated into an old lady's whisper. I tried to scream, but that was far too painful, sending me into a coughing fit that broke my heart. I fell to the ground, stopping my fall with my hands. I stared at my fingers through clouded vision, they were full of wrinkles, and veins were clearly visible beneath the skin. My nails had grown far too long, they were a nasty yellowish colour that ended in ugly, sharp, crooked ends. My skin was now a greyish white, with bones poking out beneath my out of date flesh. I felt rotten and I looked like death too. He didn't just make me old, he made me ancient, like that of a centuries old woman from before civilisation. Jipido returned with a mirror, crash landing it in front of me, I dared not look, keeping my head down in shame. However he tickled my chin with his silver hook, forcing me to look up or suffer a flesh wound, but I slammed my eyes shut, refusing to look.

"Aye, don't be like that now! Smile my pretty, you wanted this remember?" He teased me, "Said so yourself: 'Yes. I would love that' Now look what I've made yer!" He laughed with rage, digging his dirty fingers under my eye lids, snatching them open with a force that made me cry. Despite my foggy vision and tear filled eyes, my image was clear as day. I looked hideous! A shrunken skull, with paper white skin, glued tight against it. My eyes were grey like stone and small too, they were tiny marbles looking out from within this zombified body I now inhabited. I was still young inside, trapped in this prison of leathered flesh that was in much need of repair or death.

"T-turn me... back!" I begged, barely capable of speak. He only chuckled, evilly.

"Now why would I do that, ye old witch?" He asked, "Yer going to make me many a gold coin!" He laughed wildly, his voice turned deep and demonic as he revealed shark like teeth beneath his gums, both eyes glowed up a fiery orange as the tentacles from his left forearm danced freely around the air. It was obvious that Jipido was no mortal man, but a cruel sea monster, hidden under that human disguise. I was glad to have never seen his true form.

He had enslaved me, cuffing me with rope so that I could never escape. I slowly slumped through the circus tent, struggling to carry myself forwards. My head down in shame, I could see the feet and legs of other circus freaks, but I couldn't bring myself to look up and bare to witness them. Jipido was leading me through this horrifying place of sinister misery. After what felt like an hour, he sat me down inside a dresser room. I wept quietly, far too weak and decrepit to deny defeat. I knew there was no hope for me, for I was far too old and useless to runaway or attack. Jipido was the most evil of men, he made me dependant on him, I was now disabled and he was my carer. He rummaged through a treasure chest in the corner of this old fashioned room, that was a bright red with silk gowns, robes and decorations. These sights made me depressed, remembering how much I adored the circus and funfair, it's beautiful colours and sounds of joy now tortured me, knowing the dark truth behind it all. Jipido approached me with a fortune tellers outfit, I refused to wear it, wanting to hold onto the last shred of my former self. So he dressed me by force, I tried to scream, fight and escape, but within 5 minutes I was the fortune teller! I hated myself for what he had turned me into, I wanted to die!

Giving up on convincing me to preform, Jipido removed his eye-patch again. Despite my resistance, I was yet again powerless to the eye's golden charms. Without my will, my body took control and stared into his magnificent eye. "Yee will be an ancient fortune teller. Read people's palms and stroke thee crystal ball." He chanted.
"I will be an ancient fortune teller. Read palms through crystal ball." I said mindlessly, screaming internally.

Jipido led me through the circus while under his spell and I followed him like a robot, obeying his every instruction, even though inside I wanted to scream and run! He sat me down in a small purple curtained room with a table and crystal ball in the centre of it. A opening led outside to the funfair and for the full 3 hours before Pirate Cove shut that night, I was spellbound to follow out his script like a puppet. It was sorrowful when my father and brother showed up, the sight of them somehow knocked me out of Jipido's trance. "Father!" I cried. However, he had a look of disgust upon his face when I said this.

"Father?!" He snarled, "An old witch like you, my daughter?" He coughed. Father then stormed towards me, my brother also rolling up his sleeves, ready to cause trouble. "What have you circus freaks done with her!" He roared, striking me with his fist, before grappling me by the neck. My body was so frail and weak, this stung like hell.

"It-it's me, father please!" I cried in sorrow and pain.

"Bullshit!" He slapped me again, this time even harder, knocking me to the ground.

"It's me, Victoria! Please, brother, remember me!" I begged him and he snarled too.

"You are not my sister!" My brother screamed, spitting in my face. I then got a hard kick to the head, which knocked me out instantly.

When I awoke, a freakish looking clown was attending to my wounds. I immediately jumped in a panic and hit him, but he held me down and began laughing, maniacally. This creature was hideous. The clown did not wear any makeup or face paint of any kind, it was as though his very own skin was a pasty white with a vivid red nose and lips that were grotesquely large and bloated. His bare feet were stretched out far longer than any normal man and the hands were also comically large, twice the size of my head!

"Do not fear!" The clown bellowed fiercely, "I do not wish to hurt you!" He grinned.

"Get away from me you... Monster!" I cried, scrambling towards freedom, the best I could in this wretched old body.

"Donkey Jane, help me, dear god!" The clown joked, in a patronising manner. Before I knew it a short brown donkey ran into view, with blue human eyes staring up at me in panic.

"Calm yourself, woman." The donkey spoke with a little girl's voice. I was far too confused to continue screaming.

"You're a... talking donkey?" I asked with bewilderment.

"Not exactly..." It began to speak. "Just like you, I was lost child, mesmerised by Jipido's dark, evil eye of power. Forced into this life. I was just a girl, like you, venturing too far from the audience to get a look behind stage. A common tactic by the evil pirate ring master, Jipido. You don't even notice the small yellow beam in the corner of your eye as Jipido watches you with his golden eye, whispering suggestions from afar, luring you into his trap. Before you know it, you're already under his spell and soon you're one of us!" Donkey Jane moaned.

"One of us! One of us! One of us!" The clown began to laugh, dance and cheer. I was furious, before noticing the tears in his eyes.

"Oh I'm sorry, Georgie..." The donkey sighed, moving her mane to face him. She strutted across the wooden floor boards and approached the dancing clown whose movements looked painful and awkward, like he did not wish to be moving. Donkey Jane stroked her head against him and he soon eased to a stop. I stood baffled. Donkey Jane smiled weakly, looking over towards me. "One of his trigger words..." She sighed.

"What?!" I coughed.

"Part of evil Jipido's hypnotic spell!" She cried, "Other words make him do other stage performances. You'll see on

the stage when the showmen shout words at him, he performs, unwillingly with a forced smile upon his face and he laughs when wants to cry and tears up when he's happy."
"It's true!" Georgie roared with laughter.
"Oh my god..." I breathed heavily, trying to understand the unfathomable!
"Aye, it is a horrid tale what happened to Georgie boy..." A Scotsman said, walking into the scene. However he was almost 8 foot tall and wide as a brick wall, with green thick skin and fangs for teeth with two tiny black, beady eyes. This beast was a horrifying orc!
"Do not be afraid wee lass, for I was just like yee. Only I was a man when Jipido abducted me, Donkey Jane's my little wean you see?"
"E-excuse me?" I asked. The orc sighed, loudly.
"I'm his daughter." Donkey Jane corrected him.
"How come you speak... differently?" I asked carefully, trying not to offend.
"Well, wee lass, I was already a Scotsman long before Jipido, whole life I was. Me wean here was only 8 she was.

Long time ago now, wasn't it, Princess?"
The orc explained.
"We've been enslaved a long time, I'm
afraid." Donkey Jane whimpered.
"Here are lass, let me wipe them tears
up for yah..." Her father approached and
and bent down to his knees to clean her
tears. I wanted to cry too, this was
horrible.
"Why don't we attack Jipido, show him
how strong we are!" I demanded, far too
humiliated to accept this life as an
ancient, weak, freak!
"Yee can't, lass..." The orc moaned,
like as if he'd already been through
this before. "We're all under his spell,
you see? Ain't nothing we can do about
it!"
"There must be a way!" I pleaded.
"I'm afraid there isn't!" Georgie
laughed, hysterically. "We're trapped!
Forever and ever and ever!"

The North Witch

Within the North West of England there is a town named Northwich, within this place there is a local witch that not many outside of town know about. She is a beauty however, not what you would expect from a dark magician in fantasy horror. She often hangs around the busy pubs and clubs at night, standing by the bar in a beautiful red dress. She has a slim figure, curvy but athletic, perfect silk like hair that shines in the moonlight. Her eyes are a hypnotic green that no man can resist, with the perfect charisma and confidence that would normally make a woman very popular, especially with men. Yet not even the most desperate of Dans dare approach this darling. For the townsfolk know better, for this witch has an infamous notoriety for making men disappear, or turn up dead! Despite this, nobody has ever been able to prove that she is behind these mysterious events, not even the police. It's only outsiders or baby faced 18 year olds, who dare approach this mysterious woman. Luckily most are convinced of her devilish trickery and stay clear. However there have recently been some very unfortunate cases, where those unlucky few have actually ignored all well intentioned warning and followed this cruel witch into the dark woods.

There was an American fellow that was travelling through the north west of England, purposely ignoring the main cities, "to get a real feel for the British country" as he would put it. He was a seasoned globe trotter, a young man of 25 who had a lot of money, but hated cities, for he always felt like they were the same no matter where you went. His name was Daryl, a real Texas cowboy who was raised on a ranch, tending to the chickens, cows and cooking up home made meals. His father earned a fortune running their farm and the rich country boy had saved up a pretty penny to venture far away from the wild west. He soon found himself in the wild north west and ventured through Northwich, sticking out like a sore thumb, dressed in a plaid shirt, leather boots and stone washed jeans. He was an interesting guy that caught a lot of attention within the 3 days he was there. On his last night he ventured inside the busiest club in town and lay eyes on the beautiful witch in her red dress, by the bar. She turned to him, as if sensing his presence and pushed her marvellous body forwards, suggestively, back against the bar with a flirtatious smile upon her pretty little face. She looked quite odd in this disco lit club, with all the men and women dressed in skinny jeans and trendy sports jackets, with modern day haircuts, this witch looked like some fairy tale princess out of a child friendly movie in comparison. Sure, Daryl found this odd, but so was the way he dressed, so this only made him feel even more welcomed by the sparkly dressed princess.

"Glad am not the only lone wolf in this town with... unusual fashion sense." He teased, "but don't worry, sugar. I dig it, baby!"

"Oh, really now, cowboy?" She winked, "I like the look of you too, honey..." The witch bit her bottom lip, seductively. Daryl was buzzing with excitement.

"How about I get you a drink, pard'ner?"

Daryl chuckled.
"Sure... Handsome!" She smacked his backside.
"Yee haw!" Daryl grinned. The witch giggled. "So, what's your name, gal?" He asked.
"Scarlett Meadows."
"Quite the name, I must say!" Daryl winked. "The name's Daryl." He pointed at himself.
"A pleasure to meet you dear!" She shook his hand and smiled, politely. After Daryl bought Scarlett and himself some pints of liquor, he needed to use "the bathroom" as he would call it, and excused himself with the promise of returning shortly. He felt a girl like Scarlett would have men queueing up in line to meet her, but little did he know, she hadn't gotten this much attention in years! The townsfolk of Northwich knew better.

It was in the rest room, that an unlikely saviour tried, desperately, to save the poor American's life.
"You don't want to be courting with that girl, mate..." A strange man with scruffy grey hair and beard said to

Daryl by the sinks, while he washed his hands.

"What?!" Daryl snapped.

"That girl... she's bad news." He said, before leaning in closer to Daryl.

"She's a witch!" The old man whispered.

"Oh yeah, well I'm a wizard!" Daryl snickered.

"This is no laughing matter, lad!" The old man groaned, "I'm telling you, she's evil. Everyone knows, the witch of Northwich is vile!"

" 'The Witch of Northwich?' are you for real, bro?"

"Yes mate, real as fuck I tell you! Sounds mad I know, but every bloke she's pulled, ends up dead or disappears... you better call your cards and run home, lad. Before your luck runs out!" The old man warned.

"You know what... you're one nasty fuck." Daryl smiled sarcastically, before walking into the old man's shoulder, almost knocking him over. Daryl then slammed the rest room door shut behind him and sat back down with Scarlett.

"Are you ok?" The witch asked him.

"Yeah... just had some trouble."
"Oh dear!" She gasped, "What trouble?"
"Eh, just some strange man. Jealous man, more like..." Daryl swigged his pint, "Said you was a witch!"
"Well, that's absurd! Do I look like a witch to you?" She asked, rhetorically.
"Hell no, you're a beauty!" He leant in to kiss her, Scarlett's lips tasted of heaven and she held him passionately as they made out. People were looking on with fear, knowing who this witch was and that Daryl would surely be in trouble. However Daryl was naive and just thought all the men and women were jealous, he saw himself as a stud and her as an angel, hence why everyone was envious.
Suddenly, their passionate kissing was rudely interrupted as hot water was poured all over Scarlett Meadows! She screamed and thrashed around violently, throwing Daryl off of herself. The American didn't know what happened at first, until he saw the sight of that foolish old man again, standing behind her with his pint of water emptied all over her.
"You son of a bitch!" Daryl growled,

charging for the old man!

"Look! My cup is made of plastic." The old man tapped his transparent cup. It was evidently made of a thin plastic, just like all the other glasses were, to stop people from harming each other during the late clubbing hours. Daryl was shortly confused but ultimately still enraged and smacked the plastic cup of his hands.

"What's that got to do with anything?!" Daryl roared, holding the old man against the wall.

"Think about it, lad... I couldn't put hot water in a plastic cup could I, otherwise it would melt! It was cold water, meaning it couldn't have hurt her, unless she was a witch!" He explained and Daryl spat in his face.

"Get the fuck out of here, you loon!" He demanded and the old man stormed out of the club, but just before leaving he screamed: "You'll regret this, you stupid yank! I tried to save you, but I'm telling ya, that Scarlett is a witch and she'll fucking kill you!"

Shortly after this little incident, Daryl returned to Scarlett, the damage

was minor and her face was unharmed. The water did burn her right arm and shoulder a little bit however, but luckily for her and unluckily for him, Daryl was a caring person who didn't let little burns like that, stop him from falling in love with somebody.
"You alright, Scarlett?" He asked, while tending to her burns.
"Yes, I'm ok. It's nothing too bad." She winced.
"You want to go home?" Daryl asked.
"Of course, but only with you!" She embraced him again, kissing his lips passionately. Daryl fell for her all over again and really lost himself in her beauty. They left the club shortly after, both with huge smiles upon their faces, however for two completely different reasons.

That was the last time Daryl was ever seen again. Not much is known about Daryl after he wandered off into the dark forests with Scarlett the witch. However some of the townsfolk say that they heard a loud scream coming from the swamps that night and some heard his American accent within the yells of terror! Which was followed by the witch's cackle. Nobody dared enter to save him, far too afraid of Scarlett's wrath.

Several weeks later a dead body did show up, found by a local resident walking her dogs. This body wore the same clothes as Daryl. The plaid shirt, stone washed jeans (now black with water and rot) and the leather boots which were worn out and full of rips & holes. However the body in these clothes did not look like a young man, it wasn't the bloated appearance of a drowned body that bewildered people. It was the fact that the man they found looked old, ancient even. His skin a waxy yellow, skin stuck tightly to the bone with decaying flesh around the skull. He looked like a mummified corpse from thousands of years ago. In fact, many of the other dead bodies found have had a very similar appearance. The legend of the north witch has been rumoured around the town for decades, all telling the same tale:

"There is a beautiful young woman in red

dress, she stands by a bar, preying on the youth of men, so she can stay forever young by absorbing their life force. Beware the north witch!"

Warrington Warriors

In Warrington along the Bridgewater Canal, there are rumours of ghosts from the Viking age, attacking people at midnight. Many have spoken of this legend and it has spooked a lot of narrow boat owners from travelling across this area at night. One man named Barry Garland has told us about his experience with the Warrington ghost warriors in the winter of 1989.

I was travelling through Warrington along the Bridgewater Canal. It had been a long day and I was on my way home from a day trip catching up with my parents. I normally sleep through the night, but I had heard rumours of the Viking ghosts before and wanted to just get through this area quickly in case they weren't false. I was soon to find that the rumours were indeed, horrifyingly true. I heard a loud scream from the canal lane to my left, I thought about the rumours, but also believed it could've been a young woman in danger. So, I took a deep breath and foolishly followed the scream towards my doom. The waterways looked clear, but somehow my boat crashed into some kind of invisible obstruction in the middle of the water. I was sailing down there fast, so my boat was quite well beaten. I had no choice but to steer to my left and get off at a walkway. I didn't believe it had anything to do with the supernatural at first, I figured I must have crashed into something far below the waters that I couldn't see, but it was when I jumped off the boat, that I soon came to a horrifying realisation. I distinctly remember feeling two hands grab my ankles from below the water and pull me inside the freezing cold depths. I swam around, wildly paddling back to shore as these zombie arms of bone and pale white flesh snatched at my body and beat me around. When I eventually climbed back onto the walkway, I turned to see one undead Viking rise from below the murky canal to face me. The sight of this monster was terrifying! Skin loosely stuck to the Viking's skeleton like wet tissue paper, his beard was full of maggots and leaches, the armour he wore was coated with rust. He rose a broken old sword and shield towards me, ready to attack. I looked on further and saw a large legion of zombie Vikings rise up behind their leader. They all let out a terrifying roar that sounded far too deep to be human, it was more like a herd of demons from hell, gathering around an innocent victim. I fled from the undead Vikings, into a nearby forest. When I ran out of breath, I scrambled behind a large group of trees. It was dark and I could barely see, but the Vikings seemed to glow slightly under the moonlight, so they were easy to spot, as they all searched around, looking for me!

They argued with each other and roared loudly in a language I couldn't understand. Some were larger than others, with more flesh still hanging on, with more or bigger pieces of armour. They all looked equally grotesque and disturbing in my eyes though and I couldn't wait to escape these truly hideous creatures. I crawled along the ground, using the foliage to camouflage myself from being spotted, I did this because a Viking ventured closer towards my hiding spot. It must have been hours of running and hiding before one of them eventually spotted me. He swung his hatchet, trying to kill me, but I was quick on my feet and ran off further into darkness. The leader gathered his men around quickly, I didn't see them for I was running forwards and away, but I could hear them herd behind me, all roaring in that language I couldn't understand. I cut my arm and saw a bladed weapon fly in front of me, sticking into a tree. I groaned in pain, but continued sprinting anyway, raging through the forest, stumbling over logs and tree trunks. My clothes were wet and muddy from falling everywhere like some clumsy drunkard. The sharp steel of swords and spears ripping apart the clothes on my back, whipping bloodied scars into me. The pain was intense and they even grabbed me a few times, but I managed to scramble to freedom.

When I reached civilisation I barged straight into a nearby pub. I was screaming like a mad man, yelling that there were Vikings chasing me. Everyone

around the pub sat silently, starring at me, before roaring into a fit of laughter.
"There are Viking ghosts I tell you!" I cried, "Look at me! I'm covered in blo-" I stopped, looking down at myself. The wounds had disappeared, so did the blood and rips in my clothes. It was like I had never been chased by ghosts at all. I felt a fool.
"Have a pint, mate!" The bartender chuckled. I shrugged my shoulders and bought myself a strong whiskey and sat down in a lonely booth corner.

I drank alone, until another bearded bloke called for me.
"Chased by Vikings, you say?" he asked.
"Yeah, yeah... laugh it up." I groaned, swigging my pint.
"No mate, I saw them too. A long time ago. By the Bridgewater canal?"
"Uh, yeah! So..." I took another swig, "...you believe me then?"
"Of course, mate." The young man said, before sitting down with me, "My dad had his own boat, when I was just a boy, was only about... 8 to 9 years ago, hard to remember when exactly. He was about your

age..."
"He was?" I asked.
"He died." He said blankly.
"Sorry to hear." I replied, not sure what to say to him; I sat silently, staring into my pint.
"What are you sorry for?" The young man chuckled, "You didn't kill him, did you?!" he snarled.
"N- no... mate..." I stuttered. I thought for sure this kid was mental. He laughed loudly.
"Sick joke, I know..." he sighed, "but I guess that's what happens when you're just a kid, and you see fucking zombies rise from the water, dressed like warriors, charging for you and your dad, with swords and spears at the ready. Then they kill your dad in cold blood, throw him into the water, drowning him, while you flee away screaming, crying out for help!" He was shouting now, and I believed him. If the same hadn't just happened to me, I would've thought he was insane, but I was glad to know I didn't imagine the whole thing. Almost like he could read my mind, he said:
"It's good to know you're not mad, isn't it?"

"I heard the myths before, but I never believed them." I said and he nodded his head in agreement.
"Neither did the police." He sighed, "they said it was a tragic boat crash that killed my dad, and as you know; my injuries disappeared." He pointed at my clean clothes, "they only believed the part of my story when I said they drowned him, but not the undead Vikings. So his death was written off as a drowning... its nice to meet someone who actually believes me. At first people just thought I was some scared kid, trying to rationalise what I saw. I had therapy, convincing me that it was just some nightmare I had after the real accident. Then I too heard the rumours and myths around there at midnight, I thought maybe people got it from me and my ramblings. Then other men and women, even children started screaming at midnight, running through the forests, near the canal. I've even seen those bastard Vikings again, far away, but out of sight, watching other people being chased. Most manage to escape, but there have unfortunately been a few deaths here or there."

"Jesus Christ!" I gasped, then downed the rest of my pint and fought off the strong kickback. The alcohol eased me, making me feel better. The young man chuckled and drank the rest of his pint too.
"If I was you, I'd book a room upstairs tonight. Wait until the morning, before returning to the canal. You don't want to mess with those zombies, mate!" He warned and I took his advice and shortly booked a room at the bar.

That night I dreamt of those undead Vikings, surrounding me in my bed, their swords and blades ready for the kill. They sliced my neck, bleeding me out like a tap, before slashing my body apart, piece by piece! I awoke screaming, just like I do every night. Much like the young man in that bar, I've been left traumatised by my encounter with the Warrington Warriors!

Frog of Frodsham

It was the summer of 2006, me and five other friends were playing in the sun, along the Frodsham canals. We were very young back then, only 9-10 years old, well behaved and smart enough to the point where our parents were all fine with us being left alone. As long as we were altogether of course. The sun was glistening on the waters and lovely boats and ships swam passed us, delicately. I had no idea this would end up being the worst day of my life.

It all turned down hill when that hideous frog showed her grotesque face to all of us. I was dancing down the walkways, singing a silly song I don't remember. Then I stopped, suddenly staring at this freak of a frog with fiery eyes and the skin of a human, all pink, red and oily. I remember my friends gasped too at the sight of evil Froggo.
"Do not be afraid, children..." Froggo smiled, sitting calmly, "Lovely day, isn't it?"

"Uhmm, yeah I suppose so!" Cindy shrugged.
"Are you a talking frog?" Jack asked.
"Why yes I am, boys and girls! Would you like to play a game with me?" The frog waved her webbed hands. Her fingers looked strangely human, long and slender with sharp nails too. This thing looked so monstrous, yet it sounded so friendly, Froggo had the soothing voice of a caring mother or friendly school teacher.
"I don't think so..." I hesitated.
"Oh come on, Charlie! It'll be fun..." Beth whined.
"Yeah, don't be such a chicken, Charlie!" Bob mocked.
"Don't call me chicken!" I snapped.
"Charlie's right! This frog lady seems strange..." Tim whimpered.
"Ah, little Timid Timmy... Gonna go crying to mummy again?" Beth laughed at him.
"Shut up!" He whined.
"Then don't be such a pussy!" Bob snickered.
"Now, now, now children!" Froggo burped, making most of us laugh, "That's naughty language... I wouldn't want you saying

that around my babies!" she cried,
sarcastically.
"Ah! You have little babbas?" Cindy
giggled.
"Oh yes!" Smiled the frog, "but they're
just tadpoles at the moment..."
"Ah cool, I love tadpoles!" Jack
cheered.
"Well, come on into my forest, kids! We
don't bite..." Froggo grinned. Me and
Tim were wise to avoid her, but we both
felt peer pressured by Bob and Beth into
following this freakish frog into her
lair. So all of us headed into our doom,
unknowingly walking into certain death!

We all followed Froggo deeper and deeper
into her darkening forest. The sun was
sinking and daylight was fading. My
anxieties were high because we had no
idea where she was taking us. Tim and I
knew the fear of being lost, but the
others didn't care or realise it. Bob &
Beth were too arrogant to notice and
Jack & Cindy found this creature's tales
too curious not to ignore. Jack kept
asking Froggo about her tadpoles and
where she came from, why she was giant,
had human like skin and how she could

talk and so on and so on. Cindy was jumping with joy the whole journey there too.

"I'm very excited to see your babbas!" She sang with joy.

"Oh yes my darling, they're so hungry to meet you!" Froggo grinned, joyfully.

"Oh wicked! This is going to be fun!" Jack clapped his hands.

"How much longer!" Tim whined, feeling the same worry as me.

"Ah! Little Timid Timmy is scared again..." Beth laughed in his face.

"And Charlie chicken looks scared as a cat!" Bob teased.

"Shut up, Bob!" I groaned.

"We're not too long away now, boys and girls. Just a dozen more steps ahead!" Froggo cheered.

"Oh god!" I sighed, dragging my feet further into the uneven ground.

Eventually, after a long and uncomfortable trek, we arrived at Froggo's lair. By now the sun had fallen and the full moon shone high above us. The summer heat had vanished, leaving a cool chill that made the hairs on the back of my neck rise.

"Now, children... we will start with a race!" Froggo announced. Having a sprint in the dark, on this uneven ground felt foolish. Even as a child I knew this was wrong, but Bob & Beth were revving to go, trying to prove how much better they were. Jack & Cindy cheered as they got ready to flee, but me and Tim were very worried and only participated because we wanted to stick together and hoped maybe things would turn out fine and the nice frog lady would return us back to town. However, Froggo had sinister plans that were quite insidious! I felt uneasy around this monster, her polite manner, soothing voice and charm did little to calm me, but she never let on that she knew I was suspicious.

"Whoever reaches the swamp to the north wins!" Froggo ordered with a smile and before I knew it, we were all racing off into further darkness. I was jogging slowly at first, before Bob began to annoy me. Taunting me to go faster. I groaned and our chase to the finish line began. He and Beth were racing ahead all of us and I was a close third.

"Come on, Charlie Chicken!" Bob laughed, actually having fun. We were tripping over the little rabbit holes and wet mud that sent us slipping and sliding everywhere. I quickly gained on the two of them, charged to the front and was way ahead of the party. I heard Bob scream in terror, but I foolishly thought it was because I was winning. Then the ground I was running on began to sink as we entered the swamps. Beth cried out in horror.

"Help!" She begged, I turned to see her arms reaching out from the mud that was swallowing her whole. I snatched her hands and pulled up as strong as I could, but all I could manage is to reveal her face, she was covered in brown and green sludge.

"Bob fell! Deep into a hole and he's still screaming! I think..." She struggled to lift herself, "I think... Froggo lay traps for us. She wants to ea-"

"Yummy chicken..." A demonic voice burped. I turned to see the now red frog with eyes burning brightly with a hunger so fierce it was frightening. She hopped towards us at a terrifying pace.

"Don't leave me!" Beth screamed as I let go and fled deeper into the swamps. I had no idea where Cindy and Jack were, but I just had to escape with or without them. Jack screamed my name during the chase and I turned to see him scrambling towards me, his face full of fear as Froggo's eyes glowed in the distance behind us like a raging sun. Her black tongue leaped out far and wrapped itself around poor Jack. He was quickly eaten alive by the demonic frog. I wanted to puke, but had to keep running. Cindy flew in front of me, screaming in terror. She fell into a nearby pond and soon the snake like tadpoles attacked her. They had sharp teeth and ripped her apart limb from limb as she was eaten alive. The water turned red with her blood as the piranha like tadpoles spat out her broken bones out onto the surface. They all raised and stared at me with red eyes of pure lust and thirst for more blood. This time I did vomit, yet I didn't have time to clean myself, as I could hear the beats of Froggo's heart near me. She let out this roar that was so deafeningly loud and high pitched, it sent my ears ringing. Her tongue licked my foot and I tripped over, I rolled onto my back and faced the demonic frog creature as she neared me slowly. I almost died, before discovering a nearby rock that was large and sharp. I threw it at Froggo, harder than I had ever thrown, and it pierced her right eye. She held her eye with her webbed hands and let out another scream of agony. I felt something biting my fingers, it stung like hell. I looked to see a giant tadpole feasting on my hand. I punched the little monster and slammed it against a tree trunk. Red human-like blood and gore splashed from it's wounds as it flipped on the ground like a fish out of water, before easing to a stop and dying. Now Froggo and her children didn't seem so scary, however I was far too afraid to attempt to kill her. So I jumped up and ran to freedom.

When I returned to the canals, the sun was rising. The beautiful sun shone nicely against the water and the sky was a pretty orange with shades of pink. I took in a deep breath and enjoyed the fresh morning air. I thought I was the last survivor, but then I heard a familiar voice.
"Froggo is dead..." Tim said. I turned

to witness him, he was covered in red gore. Froggo's dead pink skin glued to his clothes and boots.
"You killed her?" I gasped.
"I had to!" He cried, "how can we let something like that live?"
"But... How?"
"You already hurt her. She was lying on the ground crying, I grabbed a sharp rock and beat her to death!" he trembled, breathing heavily. Not even I could believe 'Timid Timmy' could defeat such a monster! "He have to go back, burn the tadpoles!" he suggested.
"I don't know, Tim..." I gulped.
"We have to!" He snapped.
"Well, we can't go home looking like this! we'll have to clean up... somehow." I sighed. We eventually decided to wash off Froggo's blood in the canal and return home quickly.

We returned with my dad's lighter and a petrol tank I stole from his kitchen and and back garden shed. He wasn't in to stop us, for he must have been searching for us. Together me and Tim returned to the swamp, spending hours finding where he killed her. We eventually found her rotting corpse, flies, other bugs, even rats and birds were now gathering around her, eating Froggo's body apart. The stench was horrendous. We decided to leave her bloody remains there, but the original plan was to burn her body with the tadpoles in the pond. The tadpoles were staring at her, crying, making these horrifying screams of sorrow. They snarled at us when we arrived and they tried to bite us as I emptied the petrol into the water, but Tim whacked them down with a heavy stick, stopping their attack. I then took my dad's lighter, flicked on the flame and threw it into the pond while it was still lit. The water bubbled, then boiled, smoked and roared with fire. The once vengeful tadpoles now cried out in hysteria, burning alive, popping like pimples. Their blood and gore squirted out like a broken tap, they swam together, holding each other with their tiny arms, before finally dying a brutally painful death, that they most definitely deserved. We left the blazing pond alight with the dead mother by the surface of her dying children.

We thought it was over, but since 2006 me and Tim have heard many rumours of another giant frog like creature that still haunts the Frodsham canals. This one being a male that also kills children, but not to feed his offspring, no this is more out of spite. This second frog has a vengeful heart. His hatred is strong because of us! We killed his lover and children. Now maybe we're thinking we go back into the Frodsham canals and search for this beast, put an end to this madness once and for all.

It is now 2022, it has been 16 years since we first encountered Froggo and her terrifying offspring. Me and Tim are in our mid twenties now and the events of summer 2006 have haunted us for years. Not only are the night terrors horrific, but we've both felt responsible for all the deaths that have followed since Froggo's demise. It should've been obvious that she had a partner that needed to be dealt with, but the thought never occurred to us at the time and we didn't hear about the other frog of Frodsham until many years later. We've been building up the courage for years, but tonight we're finally facing our demon! Tim drove us to the old canal, we arrived there at night and just like in 2006, a full moon shone in the night sky. We parked up and exited his red pick up truck with shovels in our hands, ready to kill the last frog of Frodsham for good! Timid Timmy had changed a lot since 2006, murdering Froggo filled him with a lot of confidence, but it also traumatised him badly. So bullies were pathetic in comparison to the frog demon, however he would beat his enemies brutally, which was very strange for a young lad. He went through a lot of therapy over what happened, for the longest time we both presumed Froggo was just some shared nightmare we both had over what really happened to our old friends. Tim now rocked a beard, long black hair and was really into his heavy metal. He also dressed like a rock star too and he most definitely had the attitude. I, however wasn't really into all of that despite experiencing the same trauma. Personally I just think he tries to act "badass" to make up for his childish name "Tim" that he refuses to go by, instead he now calls himself Tommy, "like the machine gun!" he would often grin. I still call him 'Timid Timmy' just to annoy him though, but he always calls me 'Charlie Chicken' and we have a good laugh about that. Unfortunately tonight wasn't a fun one, but a deadly serious one, for we had a monster to slay!

We ventured passed the canals and deep into the nearby forests where Froggo's swamp lay abandoned. The trip somehow seemed much longer than we remembered, for there now seemed to be more thorn bushes and nettles along the way, possibly planted by Froggo's boyfriend to protect his home. We used our shovels to fight our way towards the dark den and eventually we made it. The second frog was not present. Tommy roared. "Where are you, you fucking frog!" He snarled, smashing the nearby plant life with his shovel.
"Maybe he's not here..." I sighed.
"Oh, he's here all right!" Tommy groaned, "let's burn his stupid home, then he'll show!" He roared and removed a lighter from his leather jacket.

"Wait, Timmy, what are you doing!" I gasped, as he lit the flame and began burning the trees around us.
"Flaming him out!" He laughed.
"Are you mad?! You'll burn us alive!" I screamed. We ran clear of the area and waited for the frog to show, but after minutes of waiting, he was nowhere to be seen. Suddenly the rumours began to sound ridiculous, I even began to think maybe the whole Froggo incident was just some bizarre nightmare we had and now we were surrounded by fire, about to die because of our own foolishness.
"We've got to go!" I begged him.
"No! just wait... he'll show!" Tommy cried. I looked around frantically as the fire grew stronger, we were trapped, just like before, but by a force far more fierce than some crazy frog.
"We have to go!" I shouted, pulling him away, he groaned, then ran off with me. We were almost out of the fire when we heard a horrifying scream escape from the fires behind us. We turned to witness a huge black snake without eyes reach out to grab us. Tommy smashed it with his shovel and then we heard a giant frog belch! The second frog of

Frodsham charged through the fires, his skin black and red with burns, his eyes shining brighter than the fire itself. It hopped maniacally towards us and I was terrified. Not because we were about to fight the second frog, but because of the fire that surrounded us. We both wished we could've fought him somewhere safe.

"Why have you burnt my home!" The demonic frog raged, slamming his webbed hands on the ground so fiercely the trees began to shake. Sparks of ember hit our faces, burning us slightly. The bright fires of hell were far more terrifying than the dark swamps of Froggo's den.

"We've come to avenge our friends!" Tommy roared, "we're the ones who killed your wife and kids!"

"So, you're the bastards who ruined my life!" The black frog screamed. His roars were deafening, just like Froggo's, but we held on, staring him down. He pounced for us and Tommy smacked him with his shovel, and I wrestled with his tongue that wrapped itself around my body. Black Frog gained his stance and pulled me into his mouth,

I thought for sure I would be eaten like Jack, but then Tommy saved my life by slamming his shovel down onto the frog's tongue again and again, until he sliced it clean off! The black frog's tongue loosened around me and I slithered free, the monster was wailing in pain, holding his bloodied mouth. I then picked up my shovel and smacked the frog so hard he fell into the scorching fires. It then rolled around helplessly, screaming the forest down, facing the same death of his children. We watched the frog burn to death and then to ash, just to make sure he was truly dead and gone forever, before leaving the dark forests for good. The frog of Frodsham curse had come to an end. It was finally over.

Spike Island Spiders

Stephanie had a bad habit of killing spiders, she always freaked out whenever she saw one and immediately attacked it until death. Her mother never liked her doing this though, because she thought it was cruel.
"You shouldn't do that, Steph!" She would always warn, "imagine if the roles were reversed, and a big giant spider swatted you with his big legs. I know they can be scary, but they fear you more than anything..."
Stephanie would always scoff at the notion though, never thinking such a bizarre and unreal event would ever happen.
"I hate them little eight legged freaks!" She would always bark back and kill spiders whenever she saw one.

However one day in the summer of 2018, karma had a very nasty surprise for her indeed. By this time, Stephanie had grown up, gotten herself a flat and even a husband. They had a pet dog, a golden retriever named Georgia that she would often take out for walks. Because it was the summer, spiders roamed her living space on a daily and nightly basis. She couldn't stand seeing them around her home, so she smacked them with slippers, fly swatters, news papers and burned them with bug spray. Even her husband hated how unmerciful she was towards them.

"You shouldn't do that!" He would always complain, "we should capture them and take them outside, not leave them in darkness!" he would cry. Stephanie too would scoff at his remarks.

"They're just spiders!" she would laugh, "stupid little bugs that need exterminating!"

"Actually they can be quite helpful... they kill flies and other flying insects!" he would argue.

"Well that wouldn't be too bad, if they didn't look like monsters!" she would retaliate. Her husband, Frank, knew better than to argue with his wife over trivial little things like this, so he would always let her win the argument.

One day it seemed like they had a lot more spiders than usual and on her day

off work, Stephanie ran around the whole kitchen murdering the little spiders that were everywhere! It was horrific to the point where even Frank was more than comfortable slaughtering all the little black demons, if it meant freeing his home of the pests. They soon discovered that a spider's nest had formed under the kitchen sink, inside the utility cupboard. This was the first sign of Stephanie's bad karma, but she didn't see the connection. Together they grabbed 4 cans of bug spray and lit the whole nest on fire with chemicals. Soon all the little black bugs fell like snow and Frank felt bad hearing them all wail and scream in agony, but Stephanie seemed to smile in devilish glee.
"Burn you little shits!" she would snicker, "fuck you, spiders!"
Even Frank was disturbed by her behaviour as he watched her slowly kill hundreds of spiders, with next to no mercy. Even though he hated that nest, he did admittedly feel wrong about ending all their lives. Stephanie would soon join him in the living room when it was all over and done with.
"Ah, babes why are you upset?" she asked

him, while he sat, staring blankly on the couch.
"I don't know, just feels wrong killing all them bugs..." he sighed.
"You know how ridiculous you sound?" She chuckled, "anyway... they were getting all over the place, wouldn't have been long and we would have had to call pest control."
"I know..." he sighed, "they were doing my heading!" he admitted before cuddling up to her. Their spider troubles seemed to have come to an end, but fate had one more nasty surprise up it's sleeve for spider slayer Stephanie.

A few weeks later, Stephanie decided to take her pet dog for a walk on Spike Island, across the road from where she lived in West Bank, Widnes. It was a glorious sunny day and thoughts of creepy crawlies had long since left her mind. She and Georgia left the flat and soon found themselves entering upon the island. The sun shone gloriously against the water of the canal, families, joggers and children were out and about also, just enjoying the heat. Birds chirped in the sky and swans gathered

together by the surface of the water. Even Georgia seemed happy, flopping her big ears and waving her big bushy tail around. She was a very happy dog and Stephanie was a very happy girl. Everything seemed so perfect and bright, she had no idea of the hideous horrors that were soon to await her. She led Georgia towards the path next to the forested area and felt no danger in doing so. They walked along there for about ten minutes, enjoying the sights and sounds of the island. Then she spotted a big black spider approach Georgia, who quickly ate the little bug. Stephanie found this disgusting, but didn't say anything to her dog. Then more spiders showed up on the ground she was walking on, coming from the right of her. She looked to witness a horrifying black blanket of spiders approaching her and Georgia from the field to the right. She turned back to escape, but spiders were coming on up behind her and in front of her too, the only free space she had left was the uninviting woodland to her left, so she dropped Georgia's leash and ran into the woods.
"Oh shit, Georgia!" she turned to save

her dog, but it was already too late! Georgia whimpered, and growled as more and more spiders jumped her. Climbing all over her fur, until she looked like a monster made of black spiders. They were all over the poor dog, from head to toe. They all began eating poor Georgia alive until she fell to the ground, crying in defeat as the spiders slowly tore her open and fed on her bloody insides. It was a terrifying sight that would've made Stephanie puke, if she wasn't running for her life. Stephanie could see huge spiders fall from the trees above her like snow, landing on her and biting, painfully into her body. She swatted them off left and right, as she ran deeper into darkness, screaming like a lunatic. The deeper she ran, the darker her surroundings. The sun hid behind tall towers of bark and leaves buried her inside this prison of green and brown. Soon she was lost and had no idea where she was, for the forest seemed to go on and on forever, there was no escape! On top of this, more and more spiders began stampeding towards her, she could almost hear them all scuffle and scramble towards her now, but she never turned to look to see the hideous little black monsters approach. She thought she could outrun them, and maybe she could've, but deep down inside this forest lay a dark secret. She soon found this dark truth when the floor around her caved in. Stephanie fell deep into a large hole in the ground. When she hit the bottom, she let out an agonising scream of pain, for the fall had broken her ankle. The spiders had disappeared and now she was alone in this strange little well in the woods, that was far too deep to climb out of.

Stephanie screamed "help!" for hours and nobody came to her rescue. She began to feel hungry and thirsty too, with this, panic soon began to kick in as she truly felt trapped and alone. This time she really roared for help, wailing like a burning witch for anyone, or anything to come to her rescue. Soon she was crying and desperate for attention, like a crying baby whose parents are nowhere in sight. Then she heard somebody at the top of the well, it sounded like footsteps, so she sprung to life and

cheerfully called them down.
"Help!" She yelled, "I'm down here, come down and rescu..." She stopped, as the sight of 8 evil eyes peeped over the well to look at her. Whatever had come was no man. She wasn't sure what it was, but she feared the worst. Then eight claws gathered round the well, as they lifted a huge hideous black body into the darkness. It was a giant tarantula! It came raging down the dark tunnel towards her. She could only cry and scream as her doom came crashing down. She feared the spider would end her life instantly, but what it really did was far more terrifying! The spider climbed down and gathered round her, she squirmed and scrambled around like a fly in a web, trying to escape but it was incvitable as there was nowhere she could go. Then the spider stung her, she lay limp but fully awake. Paralysed completely, yet still conscious. All she could do was watch the spider release webs from it's body and wrap them around her. It was like her worst nightmares come to life and not only was the sting paralysing, but it also stung like hell. Inside she was screaming in agony, but

her body wouldn't respond, no matter how hard she tried to fight. She couldn't even close her eyes. The spider then climbed up the well, she at first thought it was leaving her alone, but then her body began to rise behind it. The spider was rising her with his webs, while it climbed to the surface. Spider then stuck her to a big web he made high up into the trees. He left her there, but soon little spiders began climbing all over Stephanie's body, biting into her tender skin and flesh. It was like being boiled alive, yet she was still unable to fight it.

Stephanie was stuck up in this web for months, every day more and more of her would be eaten and devoured by the tiny little spiders, until she was nothing more than just skin and bones. She was alive and fully awake the whole time, as the tarantula kept her alive by force feeding her worms and webbing up her flesh wounds. All the spiders enjoyed their months long feast on Stephanie's living body. It was a glorious summer indeed.

Last Train Home

It had been a long day and Derek Sanders was on his way home from Liverpool to Runcorn. He climbed onboard the busy train from Lime Street station and was relieved to be leaving the city. He was a small town man, not used to the loud, big cities. Although his home of Runcorn was considered to be a bit of a dump, he couldn't wait to get back and enjoy the peace and quiet of a small English town. The queues into the train were horrendous, so finding a nice cosy seat at the back of the train by himself was a pleasure, until a gang of drunken football supporters joined him, disrupting his silence. It was late you see, so all of the Liverpool fans were getting the last train home and Derek really couldn't be dealing with this. Especially since he just came up to Liverpool One with the intention of landing a very sophisticated office job, however the interview he had was very awkward and he felt like it went terribly. The football fans acted like Derek didn't exist, as they screamed and

shouted about their football team's loss. Derek glued his eyes into his book he bought at the train station, the late thirties year old man was too old to be dealing with their childish behaviour.
"I can't believe that bloody ref!" One of them screamed.
"I know mate! Fucking bullshit. He was a Manchester supporter!" Another roared. Derek desperately wanted to shout in their faces, tell them how annoying they were, but he was far too shy and timid to do anything like that. There had to be at least seven or eight of these young brutes and he knew wise not to anger a drunk mob. So he groaned to himself and tried his best to read his book. It was a ghost story about a mysterious town, where a young man named Bucky Cartwright discovers some horrifying truths about said town and why it is abandoned. Derek was sure it was a good book, but he couldn't tell as his focus kept getting interrupted by the obnoxious teenagers.

It took forever for the train to start and get rolling. Derek was relieved to be travelling now, as he knew his time with the annoying football gang was about to be over in under half an hour, depending on if there were any delays or not. As the train entered the dark tunnels out of Liverpool, all the lights in the train shut off. To Derek's surprise he was the only one to yell out in anger. He felt momentarily embarrassed that everyone would be looking, but even within this darkness it became immediately clear that he was suddenly the only one in this train. Upon realising this he heard loud screams, followed by thrashing metal and then silence. He was very confused and stood up calling for somebody's attention, but nobody called back. "What the fuck?" He said to himself.

When the train exited the tunnels, everywhere was foggy, every building, tree and street corner outside was covered in white mist and he was still the only passenger onboard. The train was supposed to go to Liverpool airport and then to Runcorn, but the next stop simply read: Bilmo. The same title of the ghost story novel he bought. Derek quickly searched for his book, but it

was nowhere to be found.
Perhaps this is just a dream, he
thought. The air grew cold, icy even and
he found himself shivering. Derek stood
up from his seat and searched the train
for other passengers.

His carriage was empty, but the next one
smelt of death and he was soon to find a
gory display of broken, dead bodies all
smashed up together like squashed
oranges in a blender. It was like some
horrifying creature that let loose and
barbarically killed everyone onboard.
Derek feared a ravenous tiger, crocodile
or bear had somehow gotten onboard the
train and murdered everyone. He gulped
and ventured on further, carefully
avoiding all the bones, blood and gore
that lay haphazardly across the floor of
the moving carriage.

The third carriage was like the last
one, leading up to the front of the
train where the driver sat. Derek found
this strange as he swore the train was
at least several more carriages long.
This third carriage was much like the
first one, empty with no signs of life,

no left over bags, luggage or litter anywhere, like this carriage was brand new and had never been used before. Derek spotted the driver at the front of the train, still in his driver's seat, minding his own business like nothing had happened. Derek knocked on the window. The driver turned and Derek found it odd how ancient the man looked, with a long white beard and wrinkled face, looking and dressing more like some medieval peasant rather than a train driver. Derek knew something was horribly wrong, but felt no choice but to carry on further and learn the truth behind this bizarre adventure. The old train driver opened the glass door and smiled at Derek.

"Lost are we?" The old man snickered.

"Yeah, no shit. This train is supposed to be going to Runcorn!" Derek snapped, finally losing his patience.

"You were always a grumpy old man under that shyness, Derek..." He mocked.

"Uh, how do you know my name?"

"I know a lot about you, Derek..." The old man continued, "get off at Bilmo and the questions you ask will be answered."

"Huh, what questions?!"
"You'll know soon enough!" The old man winked, before pushing Derek back into the carriage and slamming the glass door shut. The driver returned to his controller and Derek was left hitting the glass door, trying to get in. He soon realised there was no way back inside and decided to sit down, waiting for the train to stop.

As the train neared Bilmo, familiar sights began to stand out to Derek. He noticed the silver jubilee bridge far ahead in the distance, only it had rusted over and was falling apart, it's majestic green paint had eroded into an ugly brown. The train bridge he was travelling inside of also looked like something out of a zombie apocalypse movie, and when they reached Runcorn's train station, the once modern environment now looked derelict and over grown with nettles and thorns. The train came to a stop and Derek gulped before leaving the safety of the diesel engine and venturing outside into the post apocalyptic town named Bilmo, that was still heavily coated in a thick grey mist. The air outside was even colder than the train's and as he turned to look, he was baffled to discover that the modern day diesel he thought he was inside of, was actually a rusty old stream engine that was brown and orange from years of decay. The train driver popped his head out of the window and waved at Derek, before steaming ahead into the unknown and out of sight. Now Derek found himself alone and terrified in the creepy ghost town of Bilmo.

Derek left the train station shortly after and found himself in what was supposed to be Runcorn old town, only it too was abandoned, over grown and deadly silent. Not a single light or sign of life could be found, it was like a nuclear bomb had gone off and everyone had evacuated the area two hundred years ago. There weren't even zombies or post apocalyptic scavengers to keep him company. He was in a ghost town, far worse than the one he read about in that silly little book too. He wandered through the town like a lonely ghost, wondering where everyone had gone. It was when he found the Dungeon's nightclub that a small sign of life became present. A pile of wet vomit lay just outside the old nightclub. He was bewildered by this sight, but also pleased to discover this. Even if his only company was some nearby drunk, he was glad not to be alone. Then bad memories began to play in his head. He remembered getting too drunk one night inside said club, coming onto the girls a little too strong when he was a younger lad and how he got booted out of the place by a furious doorman, before puking up his dinner outside. The vomit was in the exact same spot and he remembered the beans that were still there. Then after he had this memory the sick faded from existence, like it had never been there at all.

When Derek came across the large bus stops in the centre of town, he heard men and women screaming and shouting, furiously. He was relieved to see life until he realised it was himself, getting battered by a gang of thugs who wanted his money one night. This happened 10 years ago, yet Derek was seeing it all happen once again. He stormed in, to stop his younger self from being beaten.

"Hey! Leave him alo-"

Then the scene disappeared, along with his younger self, the gang and the screaming girls nearby. Derek was alone again and left confused and sad by what he was seeing. He thought for sure this was some horrible nightmare, walking down bad memory lane, unable to wake from his misery. Derek was surprised to see the King's Bar's doors were wide open. He hadn't checked to see if the other pubs were closed, but they all looked so abandoned and uninviting. Yet even music played inside this pub and the lights were on too, this was the only place in town that looked alive. So Derek entered gleefully.

He expected the place to be busy, maybe full of old young friends he hadn't seen in over a decade, waiting for him with smiling faces, eager to buy him a nice cold pint. However the place was still abandoned and empty, apart from one single bartender standing by the bar, his hands leaning against it, staring at Derek, as he had been waiting for him to come in.

"About time you got here!" The friendly bartender chuckled. Derek looked at the man, he was sharply dressed with a white smart shirt, bow tie and waist coat. He had a moustache too and spoke in a very polite manner, like some posh butler.

"You've been waiting for... me?" Derek pointed at himself.

"Why yes! Who else?" The bartender winked, knowingly.

"How come I'm the only one in town?" Derek asked.

"You're not only one in town..." The bartender scoffed.

"I'm not?!" Derek gasped.

"You're talking to me, aren't you?" Bartender mused.

"I'm not so sure..." Derek sighed.

"What do you mean?" He asked. Derek stared at him, blankly.

"I think I'm dreaming. This place is a nightmare, I'm asleep right now, I must be. I read a little book about a ghost town named Bilmo and now I'm here. Funny coincidence! I must've fallen asleep on the train home and sooner or later I'll awake and find myself in London or something, for fucks sake!" Derek

groaned.
"You're not too far off from the truth..." The bartender winked.
"What do you mean?" Derek asked.
"I think maybe it's about time you went home now, Derek. It's getting late..."
"But, I haven't even ordered a drin-"
Then the bartender vanished and suddenly the King's Bar was just as derelict and ghostly as the rest of the town. Derek sighed deeply and stood up and exited the old abandoned building.

The walk home was lonely and cold, more bad memories of his past came and went as he ventured further through Bilmo. However he never met another living soul since the bartender in the King's Bar. Derek decided to take his advice however to see if there would be any clues about what exactly was happening at home. It had been hours now since he had arrived in Bilmo and the longer he spent here, the less his nightmare theory began to ring true. He thought for sure he would've awoken by now if it was, so he began to wonder if he was in some kind of coma or prolonged night terror that only felt like forever, but actually wasn't. Derek lived quite far from the old town, so seeing his neighbourhood still just as lonely and abandoned, was a very haunting sign that there really was no escape from this living nightmare.

He eventually found his house and entered cautiously, not knowing what horrors awaited him. Unfortunately even his own home was left empty and derelict. He jumped into a panic screaming his wife's name and calling for his children. Derek searched the bedrooms, the kitchen, his back garden, even his attic and garage for his family, but they were nowhere to be found. He should've expected this, but now the loneliness was driving him insane. He sat down on his living room sofa, screaming and crying into his hands. He looked up and noticed his television had been left on standby. The little red light below the TV logo shone like a red beacon of hope, maybe the answers he needed were on the news? Derek took a deep breath, stood up and flicked on the television.

"Several passengers have died onboard a

train heading from Liverpool to London." The news anchor began, "this unfortunate accident occurred three hours ago. The reasons behind this tragic accident are currently unclear, we have only identified a few victims of this fatal crash. Among the deceased are: Jessica Cartwright, Sophia Anderson, Jack Carr, Sarah White, and Derek Sanders." Derek screamed and stood, staring into the TV. Next they showed footage of the crash outside of Liverpool One. It was the exact diesel engine he originally entered, he noticed red and white football shirts, hats and scarves among the debris and far in the distance, he saw his dead self far off into the background, out of focus but the body wore the exact same outfit as Derek. He shut the TV off immediately and suddenly the strange name "Bilmo" began to make sense. It was an anagram for Limbo.

Demon Dogs Of Delamere

Delamere forest, a huge and beautiful place to the north west of England. You wouldn't expect an enchanted forest like this to hide dark demons within, but I am here to tell you today the forest of Delamere is indeed haunted. Not by ghosts mind you, but spirits that possess canines. Many have walked through these forests late at night with their pet dogs, only to be shocked by an awful, horrifying surprise! I knew a woman named Danielle who walked several dogs down there one night. She was a dog walker by profession and adored her job.

"Getting paid to walk cute puppies, life couldn't get any better!" she would often say and a woman who loved her job is quite rare in this day and age. I say loved her job because one night her worst nightmares became a horrifying reality.

Danielle was only young when it happened, she was a teenager of 19 and this was several months into her job.

She knew what she was doing by now and drove her pink car towards Delamere forest, confidently with three little dogs in the back seat of her car. They were well behaved puppies, that were a joy to be around, she used to love their cute little faces and playfulness, even the way Sprinkles would jump up and lick her cheek sometimes, which was disgusting but also funny. They were mostly harmless and she enjoyed her time with them. She led them out one by one, before leashing them together. Once they were all ready for their walk and she had dog toys and treats ready, they ventured off into the dark yet beautiful forest.

The moon shone high above them like a smiling sun that guided them through the woods and lit the area in a nice yellow glow. She found Delamere forest peaceful and felt no danger in travelling deeper into the unknown. This night she took a different, new and exciting route, which led into cursed land that nobody should enter. It was here that Danielle's lovely night would turn into absolute horror! The paths were narrow and unused, almost like adventurers knew not to cross this area, but nobody had told her of the forbidden land of Delamere. It was upon entering this heavily forested area, that Danielle began to panic, thorn bushes stuck out like dangerous spikes and the area was dark with claustrophobic walls of green foliage. She didn't like this and realised the area had been abandoned for a reason. She tried pulling the dogs back to safety, but they weren't co-operating.

"Come on Fluffy, Sprinkles and Dancer! We've got to go..." She groaned, pulling the leash away, but the dogs were rooted in place like strong trees.

"Come on!" She shouted. Sprinkles growled and Fluffy turned to face her, he suddenly looked monstrous with red eyes and greasy fur that was bleeding with blood. Dancer grew large fangs and her eyes shone yellow, as she transformed into a wolf. All three dogs slowly became more and more demonic and Danielle was absolutely terrified. She dropped the leash and ran away.

She scrambled through the woods as

narrow trees stood in her way, the uneven ground was horrendous to traverse and her demon dogs were hungry for flesh! Their barks, snarls and howls were full of rage. She couldn't believe what was happening and the thorns and nettles that now dug into her body were bloody painful, but she had to keep running, scrapping her beautiful hands against dirt and bark. Sprinkle's bit her left ankle. She kicked the dog with her right. The dog whimpered.
"Oh my god, Sprinkles! I'm so sorry..." Danielle cried. Then as she approached to comfort him, he sprung to life and bit a chunk of flesh off her cheek! She screamed in horror and agony, holding the wound he left behind. She tried to stand, but then Dancer pounced on top of her, drooling all over the poor teenager. Fluffy soon joined in, ripping apart the fingers on Danielle's right hand with his razor sharp teeth. Danielle was about to die a horrible death, but then she grabbed Fluffy by the neck and slammed him against Dancer, who fell to her side. When Danielle stood, Sprinkles panicked and was about to attack again, but this time she

kicked the dog hard, sending him flying.
The dog stood up and ran away, afraid.
Now only Fluffy and Dancer were after
her and Danielle didn't want to hurt
them any more, even if they had turned
demonic. So she turned again and ran
away to a clear area.

She was lost, but needed to catch her
breath. So she sat down on a nearby
cliff side, over looking the beautiful
forest. For a moment she was at peace
and had the time to calm herself from
the constant stress. She had no idea
where the demonic dogs were, but she
could hear them searching in the forests
deep below, howling and growling for
human blood. This thought made Danielle
feel sick. She took another deep breath
and was ready to sneak back into the
woods and find her car, but fate found
her instead. Dancer and Fluffy appeared
before her, faces full of hatred, she
stepped back unconsciously and nearly
fell to her death. Debris fell from the
cliff and the fall had no end. She
gulped, terrified that this may be her
final destination. Dancer and Fluffy
left a small opening between them and it

was her only chance to escape. So, she took a deep breath and took it! Running passed the two of them was almost foolish as Dancer jumped for her already bleeding hand and Fluffy clawed into her right calve. She kicked Fluffy free, slamming him against a tree, knocking the dog out cold. Now only Dancer and Danielle remained. She ran back into the darkness, as Dancer stalked quickly behind her.

Danielle eventually found her car again, she thought it was over as she frantically search for the keys and opened the door. She quickly climbed inside and was ready to go, then Dancer jumped in behind her and began tearing at her clothes, scratching up to her neck! She punched the wind-shield so hard the glass smashed and she grabbed a shard, it cut into her already bloodied hand, but the pain gave her strength as she cut and sliced the beast. It whimpered like sprinkles and backed off, but Danielle wouldn't be fooled this time.

"Fuck off, you bad dog!" She roared slicing the evil wolf apart. It escaped her car and ran off. Danielle slammed her door shut and started up the engine, driving down the dark road out of there.

She thought it was over, but it wasn't. As she was driving, Dancer flew in front of her car, somehow outrunning the speeding vehicle. It then jumped towards her, fangs at the ready, roaring with rage. She swerved the car to one side, almost tipping the car over, but she managed to steady her steering and turned to face Dancer. This time she charged for him, racing the car towards Dancer at full speed. Before the demon dog could react, she ran it over and left the area crying.

Since then Danielle has developed a phobia towards dogs. She used to love them, had a real passion for looking after and raising puppies, but now she's been left traumatised. She always tells dog walkers to avoid Delamere forest, for they will become "Demon Dogs!". Nobody believes her though and to this day, people still enter the forbidden area that nobody should enter.

Death On The Mersey

In 1966 a crew worked onboard the Golden Yard tug boat, travelling from Liverpool Bay to Greater Manchester. It was a glorious summer day and the birds were chirping, fish danced in the water and crowds gathered around in the towns of Runcorn and Widnes that sat beside them on the River Mersey. After a wonderful day like this, with very little workplace drama, the crew onboard would never have expected their day to end so dastardly. Yet fate is a funny thing, as sometimes your greatest dreams can quickly turn into horrifying nightmares!

It all started after their hard day's work had finally come to an end. Just as Bob Garland was about to pour his brother, Bill, a pint of lager and Jimmy the cleaner one too. Michael Smith made a horrifying discovery. Captain Tony Carlsberg had ordered him to check on the engine, for he was having troubles steering the boat. It was a common problem that was usually easily fixed. However, when Michael entered the engine room, he was assaulted with a horrendous smell. He first thought it must have been rotting fish, that somehow got caught up in the propellers or something, but what he really saw, oh he would never forget. It was the other engineer, Phillip O'Brien, however he was far from alive. His body appeared to have been thrown into the propellers of the engine, jamming the effectiveness of the boat's power and steering with his deceased bones and gore. His head had been decapitated and smashed in half, his brains leaked out of his skull like a leaking bin bag and a look of pure terror was still visible upon the grotesque remains of his head. His clothes were soaked red with blood and they were feeding into the propellers, slowly blocking and killing the engine. Michael was too horrified to dare interfere, in fear of accidentally killing himself in the process. So, he turned away and ran back to tell Captain Carlsberg.

"The boat is still struggling, Michael. Some engineer you are, eh..." Captain Carlsberg groaned as Michael frantically entered the bridge of the boat. However when he saw the terrified expression on Michael's face, he soon changed his tone. "What's the matter lad?!" he gasped.

"Sir, th- the other engineer, Philip, he... oh god!" Michael cried.

"Spit it out, boy!" Captain Carlsberg roared.

"He's dead! He's fucking dead, Cap. I found him all, all, oh god, it's horrible!" Michael was in hysterics, losing his mind in fear. He cried so hard, it almost sounded like he was laughing.

"Calm yourself, boy..." Captain Carlsberg sighed, raising his hand. Michael caught his breath and steadied himself. "Good... now boy, you better show me where this happened." Captain Carlsberg said and Michael nodded his head and led him to the engine room. Along the way other staff onboard the tugboat looked over at the two concerned workmen and shortly followed behind them out of sheer curiosity.

Michael led Captain Carlsberg into the engine room and showed him the bloody

scene.
"Jesus Christ..." Captain Carlsberg moaned, "Sorry Michael, that I didn't believe you laddie..."
"It- it's ok..." Michael gulped, watching the captain. He grabbed a crowbar.
"Bloody hell, what a fucking mess!" Jeff the chef gasped. Michael and the captain turned to look and saw the rest of the crew standing behind them. In total there had been seven crew members onboard the Golden Yard. Michael and Phillip were both engineers, Jeff was the chef, Jimmy was a cleaner, Tony Carlsberg the captain and the twin brothers Bill & Ben the fishermen. Now the last of the 6 crew members all saw the dead body of Phillip O'Brien and were left wondering how he had died, but it appeared to be an unfortunate accident. Most of them never imagined that it was actually a murder!
"What happened here then?" Bill asked.
"Bloody hell, what happened, what happened?" Asked Ben.
"Just an unfortunate accident..." Captain Carlsberg sighed.
"Fuck me, that's a shit way to go!" Jeff

gulped.
"Wouldn't want to die like that..."
Jimmy cried.
"Sorry to say it lads, but if we don't
fix this mess, the engine will be stuck
and we'll be stranded." Captain
Carlsberg explained.
"Are you having a laugh?" Bill chuckled.
"He's having a laugh him!" Chuckled Ben.
"No I'm not 'having a bloody laugh!'
we've got to get this sorted..." Captain
Carlsberg snarled.
"Here are, get fucking Jimmy to do it,
he's the bastard cleaner!" Snorted Jeff.
"I guess, I'll have to..." Jimmy sighed.
"Don't worry lad, we'll help you, won't
we Michael?" Captain Carlsberg asked
rhetorically.
"Yes, Captain..." Michael agreed,
reluctantly. The other three watched as
they struggled to lift Phillip's dead
body out of the propellers.
"Ah fuck me, that fucking stinks like
shit, man!" Jeff coughed.
"We don't like that do we?" Bill asked
Ben.
"No bro, we don't like that at all!" Ben
replied.
"Let's fuck off then, lads. I've had

enough of this fucking shite!" Jeff groaned and off the other three went back to the kitchen and saloon to relax. After Jimmy, Michael and Carlsberg had removed the bloody remains of Phillip out of the way, Michael used his crowbar to try and fix the engine. Unfortunately the damage had been done and there was no way of repairing the boat. Their luck had finally ran out and now the three of them were all covered in Phillip's blood too.

"We don't get paid enough for this shit..." Captain Carlsberg sighed, "I'll grab the flare gun and radio in that were stranded. You two go get yourselves cleaned up while I do all of that." He ordered them and they followed his orders without question.

Captain Carlsberg returned to the bridge, still covered in blood, but in too much of a panic and rush to clean himself. He searched for the flare gun and medical kit, but it had disappeared. He was very puzzled and worried that maybe somebody had hidden it. Suddenly the horrifying thought that perhaps Phillip's death was a murder occurred to him, but he didn't want to believe it and shook it off as just a silly idea. He turned to the communications radio and was terrified to witness that it had been destroyed! Somebody had been into the bridge and sabotaged the equipment. Now terror really kicked in, it was starting to become alarmingly obvious that there was most certainly a killer onboard the Golden Yard tug boat, the question was: who?

"The fucking state of that poor bastard!" Jeff sighed, downing his pint.
"Not a good way to go, eh?" Bill asked rhetorically.
"Not a way I'd like to go..." Sighed Ben.
"Didn't deserve that did he, poor bastard... Good fucking man that Phillip! We shagged a few slags and that, me and him pulled bitches left and right on our travels, you know?" Jeff sighed, "I'll miss that little fucker... let's have a pint to him lads, to Phillip!" He smiled, raising his pint. The twins tapped their glasses against his.
"To Phillip!" They both cheered, before

downing their pints.
"Anyway lads..." Jeff sighed, "got to take a fucking piss and a shit. That liquor and dead body's got me feeling like fucking shite, man. I tell you!" he groaned before struggling to lift himself up.

The fat chef was a cheeky sod and decided to go outside onto the main deck and take a piss out onto the water just for fun, instead of using the toilet. He was about to get fired, before noticing Captain Carlsberg marching towards him in a panic. Jeff quickly zipped up his pants and turned to look at his boss.
"What's the matter, Tony?" He asked, casually.
"For fucks sake, Jeff! I'm your Captain... Call me Carlsberg." He moaned, clearly frustrated.
"Oh, all right... *Captain Carlsberg,* what's the matter son?" he asked. Captain Carlsberg rolled his eyes.
"I think Phillip's death was a murder... The flare gun is gone and the radio communications system is fried."
"Fucking hell, that's bad, isn't it?" Jeff asked, drunkenly.

"Yes, 'that's bad', Jeff..." Captain Carlsberg snarled, "One of us must have done it, I'm not sure who, but I have my suspicions..."

"Go on then..." Jeff asked, intrigued.

"... You think Jimmy might've done it? I mean he's the cleaner, and we leave a pretty bad mess. To be honest, you treat him like shit also and I allow it, when maybe I shouldn't!" Captain Carlsberg groaned.

"Ah, maybe... That little shit is a funny lad! I hate that fucking dick head!" Jeff snarled, "I bet he fucking killed him, you know me and Phillip, sir... best mates! I'd never do that!" Jeff was shouting, getting all worked up and angry over it. He was drunk with power and the whole situation was getting him all heated up.

"I think you're right, Jeff!" Captain Carlsberg agreed, "Let's go over there and knock some sense into him..."

"Right fucking behind you, boss!" Jeff cheered as they raged on over to the front U-berth and baths to confront Jimmy.

When the two angry workmen stormed into

the room though, they were horrified to witness another murder! This time it was Jimmy and he was left a horrifying mess. A kitchen knife lay on the wet tiles beside his dead body. The water from the bathtub still ran rapidly, creating a red fountain of his blood and gore that leaked over the edge and onto the floor. Jimmy had been stabbed in the eyes repeatedly and was covered in deep flesh wounds from where the knife had sliced him apart. Loose skin clung to the tiles like wet tissue paper and he too had a look of pure horror on his dead face, just like with Phillip. The two of them couldn't believe it. Two seconds ago they wanted to kill him, but it appeared as though somebody had already beat them to it. Jeff and Carlsberg now both felt so guilty for thinking it was him, the captain turned off the taps on the bath tub and left the area with their shoulders slumped over in defeat.

Once outside, they saw Michael still waiting to get inside the baths. He still had the blood all over him and was waiting patiently to clean up after Jimmy.

"Hey, uh... what are you two doing here?" he asked them.
"I don't think you'll be getting clean, lad..." Jeff sighed.
"Huh, why?" Michael asked.
"Jimmy's dead." Jeff replied blankly.
"Oh my god, really?!" Michael gasped in horror.
"Yes, really..." Captain Carlsberg stared.
"Why are you looking at me like that?" Michael gulped.
"Well..." he breathed, "I don't know who to believe."
"Yo- you're not seriously suggesting it was me, are you?!" Michael choked.
"I don't know..." Captain Carlsberg turned to Jeff, "maybe it was you."
"Fuck off, why would I do that?!" The chef frowned.
"You know what!" Michael interrupted, "I bet it was Bill and Ben... they always used to bully Jimmy, remember. Then again... so did Jeff."
"Shut your fucking mouth, you piece of shit!" Jeff roared, raging for Michael.
"See, look I told you! He's the killer! Him. Chef the killer!" Michael screamed.

"Stop it!" Captain Carlsberg roared. The two workmen stopped fighting. They snarled at each other like fierce snakes.
"You two are to follow me, we'll see what Bill and Ben have to say about all of this!"

The three of them returned to the kitchen and saloon where the twin fishermen were last seen, but when they arrived the two of them had left. It was certainly mysterious that they had both vanished from the scene. Suddenly the three of them began to trust each other again, as it was starting to become clear that perhaps Bill and Ben really were behind the murders.
"All right, I'm sorry lads. Looks like I was wrong about you two. I think it's safe to say that they're the killers..." Captain Carlsberg sighed.
"It- it doesn't make fucking sense." Jeff said, "they were all right lads, them two... why would they do this?" he asked.
"No they weren't, Jeff..." Michael replied rather snobbishly, "they were bullies, you saw it for yourself,

Captain. Always used to leave Jim to do all the dirty work..."

"He was the cleaner, Michael." Captain Carlsberg rolled his eyes, "that was his job."

"I know that! but, what about when we found Phillip for example?" He asked, before turning to face Jeff, "You three left him to it, laughed about leaving us cleaning that mess! 'Here are, get fucking Jimmy to do it! He's the bastard cleaner' that's exactly what you said, Jeff."

"You're right..." Captain Carlsberg sighed, "you did bully him, all three of you..." he said to Jeff. The chef snarled.

"I've had enough of this bullshit, I didn't kill anyone!" he said, before storming off. Carlsberg and Michael jumped into a panic as the chef escaped the room.

"Get after him!" Captain Carlsberg ordered and Michael rushed after him, with devilish glee.

Captain Carlsberg followed shortly behind Michael onto the main deck where Jeff stood by the end of the railing.

Carlsberg was horrified to witness the two dead bodies of Bill and Ben, both had hooks cut through their throats like gutted fish. Their blood pooled on the floor around them, proving that they had only recently been murdered. It didn't look good for Jeff the chef, for he was standing directly beside the two dead fishermen. Michael turned to look at Captain Carlsberg when he arrived on scene.

"See, look!" Michael said to Carlsberg, "I told you, he done it."

"He fucking killed them!" Jeff cried, clutching to the hand railing. Captain Carlsberg was dumbfounded, it looked so obvious that Jeff had killed them, but at the same time he was so terrified, yet Michael looked enraged.

"I wouldn't kill the twins, you've got to believe me!" he begged.

"Bullshit!" Michael snapped, "he's covered in blood..."

Captain Carlsberg looked at Jeff's hands and sleeves, they were covered in fresh blood and gore.

"I fought Michael off of them, but it was already too late!" Jeff explained, "He has blood on him too!"

Captain Carlsberg looked at Michael, he was covered in even more blood. Things were getting confusing, he didn't know who to believe!

"Jimmy was killed with a kitchen knife, remember?" Michael reminded him.

"Oh shit, yeah!" Captain Carlsberg gasped.

"You son of a bitch!" Jeff Screamed, before picking up a large fishing hook and charging for Michael.

"Stop!" Captain Carlsberg cried, as Jeff rugby tackled Michael to the ground. The younger man was just seconds away from being killed by the evil chef, as he raised his fishing hook up high in the sky to slam down hard upon poor, screaming Michael. Suddenly, Captain Carlsberg punched him, hard, knocking Jeff over onto the railing. When the chef jumped up to attack again, Captain Carlsberg quickly picked up the dropped hook and smacked it directly into Jeff's forehead, caving in his skull, a strong splash of blood hit both him and Michael. Then Jeff's face and body dropped dead, the weight of his body fell over the handrail and he went dropping down into the water below. He

was gone. Now only Michael and Tony Carlsberg remained, they were the last two survivors of the Golden Yard.
"Glad I'm not alone..." Captain Carlsberg smiled, before giving his hand to Michael to lift him up.
"Thanks, Captain." Michael chuckled as they both ventured off to find the lifeboat.

The two of them quickly found a lifeboat to ride back to shore. With a big effort, they both managed to get the heavy wooden boat in the water and set off from the Golden Yard. It was peaceful and they were both relieved to be finally free from that horrible, terrifying nightmare. Then doubts began to set in Captain Carlsberg's mind.
"I can't believe he killed everyone..." Captain Carlsberg sighed, "he seemed to be on good spirits."
"He used to bully me and Phillip too, you know. They were always jerks them three..." Michael grumbled, "he had it coming."
"Yeah, maybe. You think he tried to cover his tracks? Bill and Ben were pretty stupid and maybe he felt like

they would slip up and tell everyone they killed Phillip and Jimmy..." Captain Carlsberg suggested.
"Sounds about right..." Michael agreed, "I imagine he had a bad go at Phillip to begin with, then they fought like we did and unfortunately Phillip ended up in the propellers. He hated Jimmy too, so he probably killed him out of spite." Michael spat.
"One thing still doesn't make sense though..." Captain Carlsberg paused, "how did you know Jimmy was killed with a kitchen knife?"
"You saw his body, he was covered in stabs and a knife lay beside him." Michael explained.
"How do you know that?" Captain Carlsberg asked.
"What do you mean?!" Michael snapped, "I saw his body with you..."
"No. You didn't. Me and Jeff entered the baths, we saw his body, then we left and you were waiting outside!"
"I..."
"-In fact, we didn't see you on the way in." Captain Carlsberg interrupted Michael, "it was only after we found the body that you were there, acting all

dumb. Oh my god!" Captain Carlsberg gasped, standing up from where he was sat, "It all makes sense now! While Jeff and the twins were in the kitchen, you murdered Jimmy with Jeff's knife, while I was in the bridge finding out that all the equipment had been stolen and destroyed. You always had a hatred for them three, so you planted the knife, you knew how to press Jeff's buttons and get him riled up. Why didn't I see it before!" He yelled. Michael punched Carlsberg, before the captain could react, he was being pushed over into the water.

"You bastards!" Michael roared, "treating me and Jimmy like shit! All five of you."

"W- we were ju-just doing our... jobs!" Carlsberg struggled to speak as Michael attempted to drown him over the edge of the lifeboat. His head ducked in and out of the water, as he struggled to fight back.

"Bullshit! All you had to do was treat us with a little more respect. None of this 'Boy!' shit, none that 'He's the fucking cleaner' shit either! I was getting sick of it. Jimmy was weak, he

just accepted it, but not me, Tony!"
"Yo- you're a fu- a fucking monster!"
Captain Carlsberg roared, fighting
Michael off of himself. Michael stood
back in a panic, they now stood face to
face, ready to kill each other.
"I thought this might happen!" Michael
screamed, before brandishing another
knife from his jacket's pocket. Before
Captain Carlsberg could react, Michael
sliced his throat clean open. Carlsberg
grabbed his throat and cried, trying to
stop the bleeding. Captain Carlsberg
fell to his knees in front of Michael
and the Golden Yard killer kicked him
over the edge. Captain Carlsberg swam
around helplessly, as his blood turned
the water red around his neck. He could
no longer speak because the wound was
that deep. Shortly he bled out and just
like with Jeff, his dead body sunk down
to the bottom of the River Mersey.

Michael smiled to himself, he was
finally alone at last. It had been a
long, hard day of murder and betrayal,
but it all paid off in the end. The day
was coming to a close, a red sun set lay
behind the silver jubilee bridge. He

breathed in the fresh river air and sailed towards the red sun, enjoying the fact that he had successfully gotten away with murder.

Afterword

This is my sixth book, I really hope you have enjoyed this read. Small Town Horrors is intended to be a anthology series exploring dark horror stories set in different areas of the UK, or perhaps even the USA, Canada or Australia. Within this book, I also wrote short spin off stories relating to my other horror books; *Paranormal Homicide*, *The Town Named Bilmo* and *Realms of Solaride*. I hope this book has been a delicious taster, introducing you to my horror universe. Every book I write is connected to the last one in some way or another, even my science fiction and fantasy adventures like; *Born Without Mothers* and *New Order of Alexandria* contain elements of horror and the same world building, as well as supernatural moments similar to the ones seen within this book. I plan on crafting a huge book universe, eventually building up towards an epic finale and crossover, but truth be told I still think I'll keep writing even after this grand finish. I had too many ideas in my head however, so this book has allowed me to get some of my wilder ideas out on paper. Some of these stories may have abrupt endings, that is because I plan on further expanding these ones into much larger stories. I look forward to you reading my books again, until next time dear reader.

Acknowledgements

None of this would be possible without the endless support of my family, friends and fans who have encouraged me to keep on writing and creating stories. It has been a long and bumpy journey, but mostly one full of joy! Josh Smith has always allowed me to promote my book on his radio show, Stephen Holloran also helped me with that wonderful author interview and there are so many other friends out there who have helped me along the way too. I'd like to thank my father, Roy Wright who has always given me interesting horror story ideas and my uncle Edward Basnett too, for giving me solid business advice that has actually worked. Most of all, I'd like to thank you, the reader, for reading this book in it's entirety. I really hope you have enjoyed it and I am already writing my next one.

Horror Book Previews

Since *Small Town Horrors* is connected to my larger book universe, I thought I would share with you some sneak peak previews of my other tales of terror!

Realms Of Solaride – Preview

Prologue

In the darkest age, when man lived amongst rats, within swamps and dark forests. Where men fought with might and honour, using swords and maces. Our tale takes place long ago (1024), in a Realm very much unlike our own. Here, monsters roam the night, and fierce beasts torment their prey. As Vampires, Werewolves, Witches and Demons live amongst men, seeking fresh meat. At night, it would be most unwise for men and women to travel, unless they are well equipped, brave and mighty enough to defeat such monstrosities.

Upon the East of Solaride, a Realm named Riverfall suffers, as it is ruled by a cruel king named Raymond R. Ericsson the 2nd. Riverfall mostly consists of swamps, marshlands and dark forests, where horrifying creatures lurk. In the center of Riverfall stands Riverfall Village. The village streets here stink of stale piss, as it always rains in

Riverfall, because a horrid cloud of black, looms over the whole village like a plague. Villagers stay within small bungalows or huts. Small market tents stand on either side of the cobble stone road, leading up to Castle Ericsson. The living conditions for the poor villagers of Riverfall are foul, as the interiors to most of these buildings lay mostly bare, with little furniture, nor decoration. Most building have holes in their roofs and open holes where windows should be, the homes here look more like prison cells made of grey stone, (spare for a few homes that have been worked on by their residents) most are in need of repair, as they have been stood, since the early 800's. With this said: it is quite clear that the villagers here are depressed and poor, only the king's son and two daughters (25 year old Scott T. Ericsson, and his twin sisters, Jasmin and Carol, aged 19) live a life of luxury here. Servants and poorer working class folk, serve the great king Raymond. The most fortunate live within Castle Ericsson, while the poorest fend for themselves out on the rotting streets of Riverfall, eating rats and crows that roam the alleyways with them, they sleep on the streets and are treated with disdain, by the rest of the village folk. These beggars walk through daily, wearing rags for clothes, with starved bodies, unkempt hair and rotten teeth.

Several Taverns stand on each side of this village, all run and built by King Raymond, with no independent businesses around. Everyone serves King Raymond, one way or the other, with 80% of profits going directly to the obese king, who sits upon his golden throne, within his black stoned castle that stands threateningly tall at the end of the village. Castle Ericsson is a landmark of Solaride, as it stands to be one of the Realm's tallest castles, standing exactly 232 M in height, and 117 M in width.

Of course, with Scott T. Ericsson's royal upbringing, he has become naturally snobbish. However, he has friends, all of which suck up to him, while one young man of 21, named Ramsey Weston, serves him, by orders from the

King. Ramsey was appointed to be Scott's personal servant, after offering the King his services, in order to feed his mother and child (his wife passed away with infection, due to the Wolven epidemic of 1021) Ramsey must wash Scott's clothes, boots, swords and armour daily. As well as carry his equipment on travels and protect him at all costs. For 21; Ramsey is a rather stocky and hench bloke, he is still young and quite naive, but takes his role seriously; he always manages to keep a cool head, despite Scott's often humiliating tasks. Ramsey lives within the castle with his small family, his work is horrid, but living inside, instead of out, is worth the price. Scott, nor Raymond or Jasmin & Carol care much for the Weston family, but he shows his gratitude daily, bowing to the King, his son & two daughters, without question. As Ramsey is Scott's personal Servant, it is important, that he must always look presentable when working alongside the Royal families across the Realms of Solaride. He bathes within the finest bathhouses, and dines alongside his superior, eating the finest of dishes with the most exquisite of wines.

The Guards of Riverfall are equipped with armour made of a black metal, with golden crests, patterned into the chest and shoulder blades of this armour. They wear guarded knight helmets, with adjustable visors, to hide and protect their faces while in combat. All guards carry a small shield and sword made of aluminium, so they can quickly stance into battle with relative ease. However, their equipment is weak and meager, they cannot stand long within a real battle, but they are intimidating enough for most villagers to look the other way, when confronted.

Penalties for villagers here are severe, Raymond has many different torture devices within his dungeons below Castle Ericsson. With punishments ranging from non-disfiguring (yet painful) torture, to dismemberment and public executions. With a sadistic Dungeon Torturer, who smiles and laughs with devilish glee at his victims mercy, the villagers of Riverfall would not dare disobey King Raymond's rulings.

It is within this Village of Riverfall, that a Satanic cult stalks the night streets in secret, gathering in their circles, under canal bridges and dark alleys. They have been hatching a plan for some time now, awaiting for their time to strike! Led by an ancient Witch who served alongside the Darkest Lord Lucien, back in 112, over 900 years ago. Sahara was once a young and beautiful enchantress, but she was seduced by Lucien's dark wit and devilish charms. He and she ruled over Solaride for nearly 200 years, before the Knights from Greater Haven returned to his domain and sent the devil and his followers back to the deepest depths of hell; where they have remained since, for nearly 700 years, awaiting for their return to the land of the living. Sahara and her followers, now await outside the northern tavern of Riverfall Village. It is almost dawn, it rains heavily and the virgin Sophia, drinks blissfully unaware of the horrors that await her once she stumbles, drunkenly outside and onto the rotten old streets of Riverfall Village, as Sahara has only one last sacrifice to make, before her darling Lucien can arise once again, to wreck havoc upon the innocents of Eastern Solaride!

Parnormal Homicide - Preview

Prologue

12th of August, 1984:

Sarah White lay on top of the chaise lounge as the Psychiatrist, Peter King, sat beside her on his black leather office chair. Sarah White looked around the inside of the room from where she lay, the ceiling was painted in white, a turned off light bulb hung from the ceiling with a dark green lamp shade around it. The walls were covered in red maroon wall paper and just in front of her, there was a closed window revealing the busy streets of Liverpool outside. It was raining heavily that day; rain drops splashed loudly against the glass. The room she was inside of was a rather small square shaped room with a pine wooden door behind Peter King. The carpet in the room was patterned in beige and brown polka dots and the Psychiatrist's desk stood nearby behind him with a computer on top of it next to a bunch of files.

'Sarah, tell me more about the bad man with the blackened eyes...' Peter King smiled, patronisingly at Sarah White. Sarah was just six years old at the time wearing a plain bright green sweater and pink tracksuit bottoms with white sneakers. Her hair was curly and dark. Peter King however was middle aged with blonde hair that was greying at the sides. He wore a dark green striped suit and a pair of reading glasses. His smile was wide and wrinkles would appear around the corners of his mouth, every time he made that expression.

'He comes at night...' Sarah White answered. 'Every time I try to go to sleep at night he'll show. Mummy says that I'm just imagining these things, that I've been watching too many scary movies, but... I don't watch naughty things like that...' Sarah whimpered. Peter sighed silently in his head but managed to hide it through his forced smile. *Another kid with a wild imagination, this is going to be a pain...* Peter King thought.

'Well, sometimes we all fear the dark sweetie, I've watched plenty of scary movies and we all imagine strange monsters before bedtime, but what you've got to remember; none of those monsters are real, Sarah. All you have to do is shout "stay away!" and they will go home and leave you alone.' Peter King's smile widened. Peter's attempt at comforting her fell flat as Sarah's worried face turned into a look of frustration.

'I tried that, Pete. But, the black-eyed man, he hurt me!' Sarah cried as she pulled up the right sleeve of her green sweater; revealing several large scars on her small delicate forearm. Peter was shocked; his wide comforting smile slumped down into a frown of concern. He thought Sarah was a victim of abuse.

'Sarah, tell me now... who did this to you?' Peter's patronising tone vanished, now he was speaking to her more like a

Detective, rather than a Children's Psychiatrist.

'I told you Pete, it was the man with the black eyes...' Sarah's cries grew louder. Peter was about to approach her, to give her some comfort, but before he could do so, something strange caught his attention. Peter heard a scratching sound coming from the window to his right. He looked over to the window and saw nothing, but scratch marks were beginning to form on the outside of the window.

'He's watching us, from outside!' Sarah pointed at the window, but Peter couldn't see anyone standing outside, then a loud thud hit the window, cracking it slightly. Peter jumped back in his seat, in shock.

'Make him stop, make him stop!' Sarah began to shake her head violently; her long dark hair shook around. Peter was dumbfounded; in all his years, he had never witnessed something so bizarre. So, he just sat there, too afraid to scream, too afraid to move. Eventually the window smashed open and the once ambient sounds of street life and heavy rain exploded into the room with a loud gust of wind. Sarah then sat up straight on the chaise lounge and screamed "Stay away!" And soon enough the chaos subdued, the wind settled and Peter & Sarah were left alone in the small empty room.

'I guess your advice was right, Pete...' Sarah smiled at him through her tears. Peter King, still shaking and covered in sweat from what had just happened, turned around in his chair to face her. He looked at her, then chuckled nervously.

Shortly after, Peter King led Sarah White outside of the room and into the building's hallway. Her father, Cody White, was sitting on a chair next to other clients outside the Psychiatrist's office. The wallpaper outside of Peter King's office was olive in colour and there was a long row of other doors leading into different office rooms along the endless looking hallway. The floor was made of marble and although it was black, the glossy texture shined slightly against the ceiling's lights. Cody stood up abruptly with a look of shock on his face.

'What happened, peter?' Cody asked Peter King. Sarah White bowed her head down and walked over to her father, she wrapped her small arms around his legs as she stood. Cody looked down and stroked his daughter's hair as Peter King began to speak.

'Your daughter... I can't help her.' Peter King sighed.

'What do you mean, you can't help her?' Cody growled. The other clients sitting behind him gave Cody a weird look, but he didn't care to notice.

'What your daughter has is something... I have never seen before, she is mentally sound my friend. But something else is haunting her.' Peter King explained.

'What- What's haunting her?' Cody asked half puzzled, half annoyed.
'See for yourself...' Peter King said, as he opened the door to his office behind him.

Once Cody, Sarah and Peter were inside, Cody's jaw dropped as he saw the smashed window inside of the office room. Peter frowned once he saw Cody's reaction.
'As I was explaining to your daughter here, that her *Monster* does not exist, something strange happened... She told me the black-eyed man was there.' Peter pointed at the broken window.
'She said; he was trying to get in from the outside. Now I have never been a believer of the Supernatural, Mr.White. But, after what I have witnessed today, I now know that something... Sinister is watching your daughter.' Peter King said with concern in his voice.
'Get lost!' Cody yelled, his Daughter cried as he shouted, he instantly regretted it, but he couldn't help it. This was the third time a Psychiatrist

had said something "Supernatural" was haunting his daughter and now he finally lost his patience and snapped.

'Look what you've made me do; your idiotic claims have disturbed my daughter. I thought Psychiatrists were supposed to help the mentally ill, not harm them!' Cody yelled.

'I'm sorry, Mister White... but, your daughter seriously needs to see a Priest or... something...' Peter king tried to persuade him, but Cody refused to see the truth.

'No, I won't let you poison my daughter's mind anymore... come on sweetie, we're leaving!' Cody snarled as he snatched his daughter's hand and pulled her along with him as he stormed off towards the exit with, her struggling to keep up behind. Just before Sarah was dragged out of the building by her father, she looked behind her and noticed Peter King still standing there, his shoulders slumped forward in defeat, he smiled weakly with sadness in his eyes, as she and her father approached the exit.

The Town Named Bilmo – Preview
Chapter 1
~

It rains lightly and it is a cold night. Fog rises from the ground slowly, covering the village of Bilmo in a blanket of white mist. A single young man dressed in a grey hoodie and blue track suit walks through the derelict town, alone and spooked by the lonesome atmosphere. A full moon is high in the night's sky and it's white shine casts dark shadows across the road and pavement he walks on. A sudden beam of yellow light shines through the thick fog and the low roar of a motor running can be heard, as it approaches, the man runs onto the side of the road to allow the rusty red pick up truck to pass, he turns to watch as the truck disappears into the mist behind him like a ghost. He wanders further into this foggy old town and is awestruck by the Victorian esque buildings and houses that stand tall on either side of the road. Eventually, he comes across a small pub with stained glass windows, he can see an orange glow emitting from within and can hear the faint sounds of a song playing and perhaps even the sounds of a few men talking. He looks up at the sign hanging off the building's wall and reads; "Y Giât" underneath, there is a faded painting of a golden gate upon the wooden sign. Out of the cold and into a haven of warmth, the man enters the pub and is presented with a 1970's song about a Ghost Town that quietly echoes from the juke box at the back of the pub and the sight of a single bartender cleaning the round tables and an old man drinking a pint of what appears to be bitter. The old man is sat on his own in the corner of this rather large pub, he has a short greyed beard and a lengthy haircut to match, he wears farming clothes, a newsboy cap and a brown leather jacket with his jeans tucked into a pair of green wellies. The bartender is quite slim and slick looking, he appears to be in his thirties and has black hair that is greying at the sides, he has a rough looking face and seems unfriendly, his uniform looking a little worn out. The old man however seems wise and gentle and smiles slightly at the newcomer who has entered the bar. The Bartender sighs a little and gets behind the bar, the young man approaches.

'Beth alla I ei wneud?' the bartender asks, the young man stares blankly.

'I'm sorry, what?' The young man asks, the bartender chuckles.

'You're English?' he muses, the young man chews his lip.

'I said, "what can I do?" The baretender repeats himself, the young man searches the bar with his eyes, looking for a drink to choose, most of what he reads is in Welsh, but he eventually sees something he's familar with and orders that British lager.

'Right then...' The bartender pours him the drink and hands it over, before turning around to clean the shelves behind him.

'I'm new in town.' The young man smiles, but the bartender ignores him and he feels a little embarrassed.

'Ah never you mind him, aye.' The farmer says to the young Englishman, the young man pulls up his pint and walks over to the table where the old man is sitting, he sits down on a chair facing him. The old man sips his bitter and exhales deeply.

'So, what's a young Englishman like you doin' in a little ol' Welsh village like Bilmo, aye?' He asks.

'Well, it's a bit of a long story... simply put, I needed a change, to get away from it all.'

'Ah I see, Where you from then?'

'Liverpool.' The young man smiles.

'Ah you're a Scouser then!' The farmer laughs and chugs his pint. 'Still though... why Bilmo? we're just a little ol' village, nothing much going on round her, I can tell you that.'

'I guess I just needed to get away from the city, the loud streets, busy crowds everywhere and so on. That and... well...'

'Well what?' The farmer asks out of curiosity. The young man pauses.

'My wife died.' He smiles weakly and rolls his eyes down to his pint of lager and takes a small gulp, the farmer scratches his ear.

'Ah, I'm sorry to hear that...'

'It's ok... and thanks. I've been planning on moving out here for a while now, not specifically Bilmo, but somewhere far away and out in the country, far from anything like the city.'

'Ah I see, I ain't from round here myself, if am being honest. I've come from Rhyl, even out there in that sea side town I felt it too busy at times. So, I came out here, used my savings and bought myself a nearby farm I have. Been

here nearly a year or so I'd say. Not many stay round here long I hear. Quite strange if you ask me.'
'Anyway pal, never catched your name?' The farmer asks.
'The lads up north called me Bucko, but my full name is Bucky.'
'Ah, Bucko aye? they call me Caddock, mostly because... well, that's me name.' The farmer laughs and Bucko joins in.

The two of them drink together more and as the night goes on, the conversation turns sour as Caddock begins to pry more into Bucko's past, however Bucko doesn't seem to mind, that is however until Caddock asks him;
"How did your wife die?" By this time of night they were still the only two customers in the entire pub and the bartender had shut the juke box off and was starting to tidy up and place the chairs on top of the tables.
'It's getting late, looks like this place is closing up for the night, I better get going...' Bucko quickly

changed the subject and attempted to leave the bar politely, but Caddock was insistent.

'Oh no, don't leave, Bucko... the pub don't close for another hour or two...' Caddock pleaded and Bucko turned to face the bartender who smiled wickedly and replied with; "Don't you worry, Bucko. I'm just fixing the place up for tomorrow, we're still open til 1 o'clock." The bartender laughed and Bucko looked at the time on his watch and seen that it was only eleven.

'Look Bucko, I'll even buy you your next pint, on me, what do you say, aye? What else you going to do in Bilmo tonight?' Caddock asked rhetorically and Bucko had to agree, this village did seem rather dead and he knew he'd have a hard time falling asleep on his own tonight, he wasn't tired yet and perhaps maybe he could go for a few more beers, Caddock had seemed alright up until this point and all the while, the bartender now stood in front of him pouring out a nice cold pint of lager, that did look delicious.

'Alright... I'll tell you what happend...' Bucko reluctantly agreed.

Follow Joseph on Social Media

Facebook: New Order of Alexandria

Youtube: New Order of Alexandria

Twitter: @noa_order

Instagram: joe_noa